"Don't try me," Slocum said wearily . . .

"Don't try you? Don't try you?" the young man by the name of Bodine replied. "You'd like for me not to try you, wouldn't you? You'd like me to just . . ." The young man stopped, then shook dramatically to emphasize his point, ". . . quake in my boots because I am in the presence of the great John Slocum."

Slocum put the whiskey down with a tired sigh and turned to face his tormentor. "What have you got sticking in your craw, mister?"

"I make my livin' with my gun now, and I figured if I killed the great John Slocum in a fair fight, why, the price of my gun is going to go up."

His smile quickly turned to an angry snarl. "Draw, Slocum!" he shouted, going for his own gun even before he issued the challenge.

Bodine was quick, quicker than anyone else this town had ever seen. But midway through his draw he realized he wasn't quick enough. The arrogant confidence in his eyes was replaced by fear, then acceptance of the fact that he was about to be killed.

The two pistols discharged almost simultaneously, but Slocum had been able to bring his gun to bear and his bullet plunged into Bodine's chest. The bullet from Bodine's gun smashed the glass that held Slocum's drink, sending up a shower of whiskey and tiny shards of glass.

"Looks like I'm going to need a refill, Ed. . . ."

DON'T MISS THESE
ALL-ACTION WESTERN SERIES
FROM THE BERKLEY PUBLISHING GROUP

THE GUNSMITH by J. R. Roberts
Clint Adams was a legend among lawmen, outlaws, and ladies. They called him . . . the Gunsmith.

LONGARM by Tabor Evans
The popular long-running series about Deputy U.S. Marshal Long—his life, his loves, his fight for justice.

SLOCUM by Jake Logan
Today's longest-running action Western. John Slocum rides a deadly trail of hot blood and cold steel.

BUSHWHACKERS by B. J. Lanagan
An action-packed series by the creators of Longarm! The rousing adventures of the most brutal gang of cutthroats ever assembled—Quantrill's Raiders.

DIAMONDBACK by Guy Brewer
Dex Yancey is Diamondback, a Southern gentleman turned con man when his brother cheats him out of the family fortune. Ladies love him. Gamblers hate him. But nobody pulls one over on Dex . . .

WILDGUN by Jack Hanson
The blazing adventures of mountain man Will Barlow—from the creators of Longarm!

TEXAS TRACKER by Tom Calhoun
Meet J. T. Law: the most relentless and dangerous manhunter in all Texas. Where sheriffs and posses fail, he's the best man to bring in the most vicious outlaws—for a price.

JAKE LOGAN

SLOCUM, A JURY OF ONE

J

JOVE BOOKS, NEW YORK

SLOCUM, A JURY OF ONE

A Jove Book / published by arrangement with
the author

PRINTING HISTORY
Jove edition / October 2002

Copyright © 2002 by Penguin Putnam Inc.

ISBN: 0-515-13389-2

A JOVE BOOK®
Jove Books are published by The Berkley Publishing Group,
a division of Penguin Putnam Inc.,
375 Hudson Street, New York, New York 10014.
JOVE and the "J" design
are trademarks belonging to Penguin Putnam Inc.

PRINTED IN THE UNITED STATES OF AMERICA

10 9 8 7 6 5 4 3 2 1

1

"Oyez, oyez, oyez, this here court of Sublette County, Pinedale, Wyoming, will now come to order, the Honorable Judge Daniel Heckemeyer presiding. All rise."

John Slocum stood with the others. There was a scrape of chairs, a rustle of pants, petticoats, and skirts, as the spectators in the courtroom stood. A spittoon rang as one male member of the gallery made a last-second, accurate expectoration of his tobacco quid.

The gallery was limited to fifty spectators, and tickets for attendance were highly prized. The two defendants, Angus Dingo and Flatnose Nelson had murdered Ned and Kathy Caulder. The Caulders owned a small ranch near Pinedale. They were known as good and generous neighbors, always the first to arrive at a barn raising, the first to offer help when someone was in trouble.

There was no question as to who did it. Ned managed to live long enough to write a note, explaining that their assailants were two men he had hired, not because he needed the help, but because he thought they were down on their luck and needed the job.

Judge Heckemeyer was a robust man, with a square face and piercing blue eyes, so his presence was immediately felt. He moved quickly to the bench, then sat down.

"Be seated."

The gallery sat, then watched as the two defendants were brought in. The case for the prosecution was swift and simple. Two witnesses testified that they had seen Angus Dingo and Flatnose Nelson at the Caulder ranch on the very day of the murder.

The defense had a witness as well, a man named Kelly O'Riley, who claimed that he had come by the Caulder ranch just before noon, and that when he left, Dingo and Nelson left with him. According to Kelly, the Caulders were still alive when they left.

In his instructions to the jury, Judge Heckemeyer said that Kelly O'Riley was not a very reliable witness, whereas the two witnesses for the prosecution, a man and his wife, were known citizens of good character. Judge Heckemeyer also reminded the jury that unless an overwhelming preponderance of evidence was found to the contrary, the letter Ned Caulder had written would be regarded as true.

To no one's surprise, the jury found Dingo and Nelson guilty.

The court-appointed attorney, as amicus curiae, objected to having both men tried at the same time, but Judge Heckemeyer denied the objection.

Less than an hour after Judge Heckemcyer entered the courtroom, the two men stood convicted for a capital crime.

"Bailiff, would you position the prisoners before the bench for sentencing, please?" Judge Heckemeyer asked.

"Yes, Your Honor."

The two men were brought before the bench. Though Flatnose Nelson stood with his head bowed contritely, Dingo stared defiantly at the judge.

"Get it over with, old man," Dingo said. "I ain't got all day." He giggled at his own joke.

"Abner Nelson and Angus Dingo," Judge Heckemeyer began. "In the morning the sun will rise over these beautiful Wyoming hills and move into the canyons and draws to push away the last remnants of purple haze. The air will be clean and fresh at the start of God's new day. The fish will jump in the ponds, the frogs will croak on the banks of the rivers and streams, the dew will sparkle in a thousand brilliant colors, but you two won't see any of this.

"By noon, the sun will have filled the sky with its golden light, but you two men won't be sitting down to lunch.

"The birds will sing, squirrels will scamper among the aspens, and honeybees will drink the sweet nectar of wildflowers, but you will not be here to enjoy any of these things.

"You will not be here because I hereby order the marshal of Sweetwater County to lead you to the gallows at ten o'clock on tomorrow morning. There, the hangman will put a knotted noose around your neck and pull the trapdoor lever, thereby dropping your filthy, raping, murdering, stealing carcasses ten feet, where you will both break your necks or die by strangulation. Your bodies will swing in the breeze while the townsfolk look at, and revile your miserable corpses. Then your worthless bodies will be cut down, placed in crude pine boxes, and buried six feet underground where the worms and maggot can have free rein over what is left of your mortal bodies, you worthless sons of bitches."

The gallery began cheering and applauding, not only over the judge's poetic words, but also over the fact that the two were going to get their just rewards. Slocum was as happy over the outcome as anyone in the entire town.

Slcoum's connection was strictly personal. Ned Caulder had been a particularly good friend of John Slocum's. Ned had come to married life, and the ranching business, by a series of misadventures. Like many other a wanderer, Ned had ridden on both sides of the law, sometimes wearing a badge, sometimes fleeing from those who wore the badge. His success in making a new, stable life, was an inspiration to those who now found themselves longing for something more, something better. Ned and Kathy were proof that such fantasies do come true.

In killing Ned and Kathy Caulder, Dingo and Nelson had robbed such men of their fantasies, had taken away their great hope. Slocum had no such fantasies, nor did he need them to want justice done in this case. Ned Caulder was his friend, and that was all the impetus he needed to want to see justice done.

Flatnose Nelson rolled his third quirly of the morning as he paced back and forth in the eight feet of cell block. He wasn't looking at anything in particular, he was just staring straight ahead as if the wall might melt away on his next turn and he could walk right through. Angus Dingo lay on his back on the bunk, an arm thrown across his eyes.

Outside the cell, the sound of the pulley straining with the sand-weight floated across the town square and in through the tiny barred window. As the weight slammed down against the trapdoor, Flatnose Nelson jumped, and let out a little cry of alarm. Dingo laughed, a dry, bitter laugh that could have come from hell.

"Don't you fret none, Flatnose," Dingo said. "They're just greasing the door to hell for you."

"Dammit to hell, Dingo, you sure got us in a fix this time. I thought you said if we kilt both of them, there wouldn't be no witnesses."

"You're the one that didn't kill Caulder," Dingo said. "If you had done what I told you to do, he wouldn't have lived long enough to leave a letter, like he done."

Nelson put his hand to his neck. "I never thought I'd be hung. I figured I might get shot someday, but I never thought I'd get hung."

"You ain't hung yet," Dingo said.

A glimmer of hope flitted across Nelson's face. "You mean we ain't goin' to be hung?"

"I'm just sayin', we ain't hung yet," Dingo repeated cryptically.

Outside they continued to test the device, and, over and over again, the trapdoor would spring and the rope sing on the pulley before the sandbag hit the ground with a violent thud.

Nelson let out a small whimper, then he threw his cigarette on the dirt floor of the cell and ground it to powder under his bootheel.

Dingo laughed, a dry, evil laugh.

Slocum noticed that the spectacle of a public hanging had drawn visitors from miles around. As a result, there were a lot of strange faces in the town, most of whom were gathered on the square. This wasn't the first hanging Slocum had ever seen, but it had been a while since he had looked forward to one as much as he was looking forward to this one.

The gallows stood in the center of town, its grisly shadow stretching under the morning sun. It was not quite nine o'clock, but the crowd was already thick, jostling for position. Heckemeyer had ordered the hanging to commence at ten sharp, so the people could get back to their business and talk over their lunch about justice being done.

Several hundred people were gathered around the gallows, men in suits, shirtsleeves, and overalls, women in long dresses and bonnets, children threading in and out of the groups as they chased one another around the square. A few enterprising vendors passed through the crowd selling lemonade, beer, and sweet rolls. In one corner of the yard a black-frocked preacher stood on an overturned box, taking advantage of the situation to deliver a fiery sermon. The man was of average height and build, with a full head of thick black hair. Standing on the box, he jabbed his finger repeatedly toward the gallows as he harangued the crowd.

"In a few moments two men are going to be hurtled into eternity . . . sent to meet their Maker with blood on their hands and sin in their hearts."

He waggled his finger at the crowd. "And hear this now! Them two sinners is going to be cast into hell because neither one of them has repented of his sins.

"It's too late for them, brothers 'n' sisters. They are doomed to the fiery furnaces of hell, doomed to writhe in agony forever!"

Some of those who were close enough to hear the preacher shivered involuntarily at his powerful imagery and looked toward the gallows. One or two of them touched their necks fearfully, and a few souls, perhaps weak on willpower, sneaked a drink from a bottle.

"It's too late for them, but it's not too late for you! Repent! Repent now, I say, for the wages of sin is death and eternal perdition!"

The preacher's voice carried well and was certainly heard by the two men in the holding cell. At the window of the cell, a face would sometimes appear, look nervously through the bars at the crowd, then withdraw to the gloomy shadows within. A couple of young boys approached the cell and tried to peer in through the window, but a woman called out to them and they returned to the crowd.

"Flatnose, will you sit down? You're as nervous as a whore in church," Dingo growled.

"Don't you think I have a right to be nervous? They're about to hang us out there."

There was the sound of keys, rattling in the lock of the door. "Oh! They're coming for us!" Flatnose said, his voice breaking with panic.

Dingo sat up on the side of his bunk and looked toward the door. A broad smile spread across his face.

"Hello, O'Riley," he said.

"Better hurry," O'Riley said. "If someone sees the guard with his throat cut, they're going to know something is going on."

"You got the horses?"

"Two of them out back."

"Just two?" Nelson asked. It was obvious that he feared he was being left behind.

"I'm not going with you," O'Riley said. "I'm going back into the crowd. I'll be as surprised as everyone else when they don't bring you out. Better get going."

"Yeah," Dingo said.

Kelly O'Riley watched as Angus Dingo and Flatnose Nelson snuck out the back, mounted their horses, then rode quietly and unobserved down the alley toward the edge of town. Neither of them said thanks, nor did O'Riley expect them to. O'Riley hurried back to the square, then stood in the midst of the crowd, listening to the preacher's harangue.

Slocum walked over toward the bank and, leaning down, looked in through the window to check the time. It was five minutes after ten. In his sentencing, Judge Heckemeyer had been very specific about the time. He had said they would be hanged at ten o'clock. And, even if the bank clock was a few minutes fast, the prisoners still should have been brought out by now. The judge's sentence would have to be read, they would each be given a chance to say a last word, the noose had to be put around their necks . . . all that would take up a few minutes, so by rights, they should have been brought out before ten.

"Escaped . . . ," Slocum heard someone say as he stepped back out into the street.

Even before the word was verified, though, Slocum knew that something had gone drastically wrong. Like a wind blowing through a field of tall grass, a wave passed through the crowd, only this was a wave of confusion, frustration, and ultimately, anger.

"Escaped." He heard the word again.

Then he heard the complete sentence. "Deputy Morgan is dead. Dingo and Nelson have escaped!"

Slocum knew Deputy Morgan. It had been Slocum and Morgan who found and captured Dingo and Nelson after the two outlaws murdered Ned and Kathy Caulder.

"I almost hate to take the bastards in," Morgan had told Slocum.

"Why is that?"

"Because there is always the chance they might get away. If I had my way, we'd just shoot these sorry sonsofbitches now."

"Shooting is too good for them," Slocum said. "I want to see them hang."

Now, Deputy Morgan was dead and his words were all too prophetic. He was right. They should've shot the bastards when they caught them. But Slocum was right as well: Shooting was too good for them. If ever there was anyone who should be hanged, it was Angus Dingo.

2

When Slocum arrived in Boulder, Wyoming, he saw a banner stretched across the street which read, HORSESHOE PITCHING CONTEST.

The hollow clumping sound of his horse's hooves was interrupted by a clang, then a cheer.

"You're going to be workin' against a leaner there, Dobbs," someone in the crowd said. "Better be careful you don't knock it down so that it becomes a ringer."

"You boys don't worry none about ole' Andrew Dobbs," someone said. By then, Slocum was even with the contest, and he saw that the speaker was Dobbs himself, preparing to throw a horseshoe. Dobbs, who was short, round, and bald-headed, threw the horseshoe and knocked the leaner aside. His own horseshoe looped around the stub, the horseshoe spinning before it fell.

"Damn, Dobbs, you ought to give up barberin' and do nothin' but pitch horseshoes," someone said in admiration.

"You find me a way to make a livin' doin' that, and I will," Dobbs replied. The others laughed, then Dobbs tossed again and they cheered as he threw another ringer.

Slocum continued on past the contest, observing, as he did so, the corners and rooftops of buildings, checking doorways and kiosks . . . anyplace that might provide concealment for a would-be shooter.

A moment later he pulled up in front of the saloon, dismounted, went inside, stepped up to the bar, and slapped a silver coin down in front of him.

The sound of the coin made the saloonkeeper look around. The man waiting to be served looked like a piece of rawhide. He was thin, with a craggy face and a shock of sun-weathered hair, but it was his eyes that made him come alive. Though deeply lined from years on the plains, they flashed with a fire that had been kindled years ago and still burned, stoked by experiences that would fill the lifetimes of three men.

"John Slocum," the bartender said, smiling at him. "I haven't see you since . . . when? Abilene? How are things going with you?"

"Hello, Ed," Slocum said, dredging up the barkeep's name from somewhere deep in the recesses of his mind. The Abilene reference helped.

The broadening smile on the bartender's face showed how pleased he was to be remembered by this man. Ed shoved the coin back to Slocum. "First one is on me, John. Old friends who drop by always get the first one free."

"Thanks," Slocum said.

"I heard what happened to Ned Caulder," Ed said. "He was a good man."

"Yeah," Slocum replied without elaboration.

"And they say the son of a bitch who killed him . . . Dingo, was it? They say he got away, beat the hangman by no more'n ten or fifteen minutes."

"That's what they say," Slocum replied.

"Yeah, well, I hope they find the bastard," Ed concluded.

Ed was good at his job, and one of the attributes of being a good bartender was the ability to determine when a customer wanted to talk and when a customer would rather be left alone. It was obvious that Slocum just wanted to enjoy his drink in peace, so Ed slid on down to the far end of the bar and began polishing glasses.

When John Slocum had ridden into town a few minutes earlier, news of his arrival spread quickly. Old men held up their grandsons to point him out as he rode by, so that the young ones could remember this moment, and, many years from now, tell their own grandchildren about it. Those grandchildren would ultimately tell their grandchildren that their grandfather had once seen John Slocum, so that the legend of the man would span seven generations.

Slocum had earned this not-always-welcome notoriety because of his prowess with a Colt. Lean and wiry, he was as quick as a thought and deadlier than a rattlesnake. Many a would-be shootist had gone down before his gun.

Slocum picked up his drink, then slowly surveyed the interior of the saloon. It was typical of the many he had seen over the past several years. Wide, rough-hewn boards formed the plank floor, and against the wall behind the long, brown-stained bar was a shelf of whiskey bottles, their number doubled by the mirror they stood against. Half a dozen tables, occupied by a dozen or so men filled the room, and tobacco smoke hovered in a noxious cloud just under the ceiling. It was now twilight, and as daylight disappeared, flickering kerosene lanterns combined with the smoke to make the room seem even hazier.

During the past several years these kinds of surroundings had become John Slocum's heritage. The saloons, cow towns, stables, dusty streets, and open prairies he had encountered had redefined him. He could not deny them without denying his own existence, and yet, with all that was in him, he wished it was not so.

At the opposite end of the bar stood a young man wearing a black hat with a silver headband, from which protruded a small red feather. Hanging low in a quick-draw holster on the right side of a bullet-studded belt was a silver-plated Colt .44, its grip inlaid with mother-of-pearl. The man was slender, with dark hair and dark eyes, and there was a gracefulness and economy of motion about the way he walked and moved.

Watching Slocum in the mirror, the young man tossed his drink down and wiped the back of his hand across his mouth. Then he turned to look at Slocum.

"Hey, you."

Slocum did not turn.

"I'm talkin' to you, old man."

Slocum looked at him and saluted him silently with his drink. He knew from the tone of the young man's voice, though, that he wasn't being offered a simple greeting.

"You're John Slocum, are you?"

Slocum didn't answer.

"I heard the barkeep call you by that. John Slocum, he said. Is that you?"

"I'm Slocum."

"I've got a bone to pick with you, Mr. John Slocum, Mr. famous . . . gunfighter." He set the last word apart from the rest of the sentence, and said it with a sneer.

"Mister, I'm worn and tired, and over the years I've had about a bellyfull of putting up with people like you. Don't try me," Slocum said, wearily.

"Don't try you? Don't try you?" the young man replied.

He turned to address the others. The saloon had grown deathly still now as the patrons sat quietly, nervously, and yet titillated, too, by the life-and-death drama that had suddenly begun to unfold in front of them. "You'd like for me not to try you, wouldn't you? You'd like me to just . . ." The young man stopped, then shook, dramatically to emphasize a point . . . "quake in my boots because I am in the presence of the great John Slocum."

Slocum put the whiskey down with a tired sigh and turned to face his tormentor. "What have you got sticking in your craw, mister?" he asked. "Have I killed a brother, a friend, your old man, perhaps?"

"No, nothin' like that," the young man answered. "It's just that I make my livin' with my gun now, and I figured if I killed the great John Slocum in a fair fight, why, the price of my gun is going to go up."

"What is your name?"

"The name is Bodine. Kyle Bodine. I reckon you've heard of me."

"I've heard of you," Slocum said.

Bodine's smile broadened. "Yeah? What have you heard?"

"I've heard that you are a pissant, trying to make it in a man's world."

Bodine's smile quickly turned to an angry snarl. "Draw, Slocum!" he shouted, going for his own gun even before he issued the challenge.

Bodine was quick, quicker than anyone else in this town had ever seen. But midway through his draw Bodine realized he wasn't quick enough. The arrogant confidence in his eyes was replaced by fear, then acceptance of the fact that he was about to be killed.

The two pistols discharged almost simultaneously, but Slocum had been able to bring his gun to bear and his bullet plunged into Bodine's chest. The bullet from Bodine's gun smashed the glass that held Slocum's drink, sending up a shower of whiskey and tiny shards of glass.

Looking down at himself, Bodine put his hand over his wound, then pulled it away and examined the blood that had pooled in his palm. When he looked back at Slocum, there was an almost whimsical smile on his face.

"Damn," he said. "You're good. I thought I could beat you. I really thought . . ." His sentence ended with a cough, then he fell back against the bar, making an attempt to grab onto the bar to keep himself erect. The attempt was unsuccessful, and Bodine fell on his back, his right arm stretched out beside him. His silver-plated, mother-of-pearl-handled pistol was still connected to him only because his forefinger was hung up in the trigger guard. The black hat, with its silver band and red feather had rolled across the floor and now rested in a half-filled spittoon. The eye-burning, acrid smoke of two discharges hung in a gray-blue cloud just below the ceiling.

Slocum turned back to the bar where pieces of broken glass and a small puddle of whiskey marked the spot of his drink.

"Looks like I'm going to need a refill, Ed," Slocum said.

"Sure thing, John. Coming right up," Ed said, pulling the cork on a new bottle and, with shaking hands, pouring the liquor into another glass.

Behind Slocum the silence was broken as everyone discussed what they had just seen. Slocum was only halfway through his drink when the town marshal and two of his deputies arrived.

"What happened here?" the marshal asked.

The question wasn't directed to anyone in particular, so everyone started answering at once, availing themselves of the first opportunity to tell a story they would be telling for the rest of their lives.

"Hold it, hold it!" the marshal said, holding up his hands. "Don't everyone talk at once." The marshal looked over toward the bartender. "Ed, did you see what happened?"

"Bodine tried to brace Slocum."

"Bodine started the fight?"

"Come on, Marshal, you know Bodine. Or, I guess I should say, knew him."

"Ed's tellin' it like it is, Marshal," one of the saloon patrons said. "All Slocum done was buy hisself a drink and next thing you know, Bodine was jerkin' a cinch into him."

"What you mean is, Bodine was *trying* to jerk a cinch into him," one of the others said. "Only, he didn't get very far."

The marshal stroked his chin as he looked at Bodine. Death had made the young, would-be gunman's face appear slack-jawed and distorted.

"Bodine was trying to make a name for himself, wasn't he?" the marshal asked.

"Looks that way."

The marshal walked down the bar to Slocum, who was calmly sipping his whiskey.

"Mr. Slocum, the name is Tom Drew. I'm the marshal here; town marshal, not county."

"Marshal," Slocum said with a slight nod.

Marshal Drew looked back toward Bodine. "I reckon you run across punks like Bodine, here, more times than you can count, don't you?"

"From time to time," Slocum said. "Most men have more sense than he did. And less guts," he added in a begrudging acknowledgment of Bodine's misplaced courage.

"Yes, well, here's what I'm getting at, Mr. Slocum. You planning on staying in my town long?"

"I'm here to meet someone."

"Who, if I may ask? Perhaps I can help you find him."

"I don't need to find him," Slocum said. "He'll find me."

"And then?"

"Then, I thought I might have supper and maybe spend a night in a real bed before going on."

It was obvious that Drew wanted to tell Slocum to go on, now, don't meet anyone, don't wait for his supper, and don't take a room. But, it was equally obvious that the marshal was afraid to confront John Slocum. Instead, he stroked his chin and jaw, then nodded.

"Yes, well, I'm sure you'll find everything you need in our fair town," he said.

A tall, very gaunt-looking man dressed in black tails and a high hat, came in then. Two other men were with him.

"Well, Abernathy, I see it didn't take you long to get here," the marshal said. "Our undertaker," he added, speaking to Slocum.

"Oh dear," Abernathy said. "It's young Mr. Bodine."

"Get him out of here," the marshal said.

Abernathy nodded toward his two associates, and they picked the body up and carried him out. Immediately after the body was moved, a Mexican who worked for Ed arrived with a bucket of soapy water and a stiff brush. He began cleaning up the blood.

"Mr. Slocum, I do hope the rest of your stay is more peaceful," the marshal said as he and his two deputies followed Abernathy out of the saloon.

Just as the marshal was leaving, another man came in. He stopped just inside the batwing doors, and looked around for a moment. Seeing Slocum at the bar, he walked over to join him.

"Hello, Paul," Slocum said.

"John," Paul replied. Paul nodded toward the front door. "I just saw some galoot being taken out. What happened?"

"He had something to prove."

"I take it he didn't prove it."

Slocum didn't answer, but held up his finger toward Ed as a signal that he wanted another drink.

"Yes, sir, Mr. Slocum. Right away," Ed said, bringing the bottle toward Slocum's glass.

"No, a new glass," Slocum said.

Ed poured the drink in a new glass, and Slocum handed it to Paul.

"Thanks," Paul said, taking the drink and tossing it down.

"Do you have anything for me?" Slocum asked.

Paul smiled. "I found 'em," he said.

"Where?"

"Well, I didn't actually find them. But I know where they are planning to be for the next couple of days. It's a place called Whiskey Wells. You ever heard of it?"

"Yeah, I've heard of it."

"They say Angus Dingo is riding a black gelding with a white blaze on its face and a white stocking on the right rear leg. Flatnose Nelson, the fella with him, is riding a roan."

"Thanks, Paul."

"No thanks needed," Paul replied, holding up his hand. "Ned and Kathy was my friends, too. I'd like nothing better in the world than to see the sonofabitches who killed them, get theirs."

"Whiskey Wells?" the woman said. "What, pray tell, is Whiskey Wells?"

"It's a town, ma'am. Some west of here."

"Then please arrange passage."

"Yes, ma'am."

3

After six hours on a bumping, rattling, jerking, and dusty stagecoach, the passengers' first view of Whiskey Wells was often a bitter disappointment. Sometimes visitors from the East had to have the town pointed out to them, for from this perspective, and at this distance, the settlement looked little more inviting than another group of the brown hummocks and hills common to this country.

The town had been started by a man named George Matson. He was a saloonkeeper and would-be entrepreneur who had high hopes and lofty ambitions. But Matson was shot down in the street of his own town, and the drunken cowboy who killed him was himself strung up before the sun set that very day. Now, the town that Matson had founded was dying on the plains, probably doomed to extinction within another fifty years.

John Slocum stopped on a ridge just above the road leading into Whiskey Wells. He took a swallow from his canteen and watched the stage as it started down from the pass, into the town. Then, corking the canteen, he slapped his legs against the side of his horse and sloped down the long ridge. Although he was actually farther away from town than the coach, he would beat it there, because he was going by a more direct route.

A small sign just on the edge of town read: WHISKEY WELLS, POPULATION 94, A GROWING COMMUNITY.

The weathered board and faded letters of the sign indicated that it had been there for some time, perhaps posted even before Matson was killed, erected when there was still optimism for the town's future. Slocum doubted that there were ninety-four residents in the town today, and he was positive that it was no longer a growing community.

John Slocum was a loner, a man whose home was the saddle, whose last address was a puff of dust carried on the hot, desert wind. And because such men had few friends, the value of those he did have was greatly increased. Ned Caulder had been such a friend. Slocum's visits to Ned and Kathy were few and far between, but going to the Caulder ranch had always been one of the closest things to going home John Slocum could experience. Slocum knew who killed them, because Ned had lived long enough to leave a brief note, telling what had happened.

By the time someone reeds this leter I will be ded. I was shot by 2 men whose names are Angus Dingo and Flatnose Nelson. They was werking for me castrating caves. They stoled the money I had from the sale of them caves, then they shot me. When I come to I seen they had also kilt Kathy. I do not think I can hode on much longer. I hope whoever finds this leter will find Dingo and Nelson and make them pay for what they dun.

Ned was found dead, slumped across the kitchen table, the note clutched tightly in his hand. Kathy was also dead, and the condition of her body indicated that she had been raped and brutalized before she was murdered.

As Slocum rode into Whiskey Wells he surveyed the little town closely. In addition to the false-fronted shanties that lined each side of the street, there were a few sod buildings, and even some tents, straggling along for nearly a quarter of a mile. Then, just as abruptly as the town started, it quit, and the prairie began again.

In the winter and spring the street was a muddy mire, worked by the horse's hooves and mixed with their droppings, so that it became a stinking, sucking, pool of ooze. In the winter it was often frozen solid, while in the summer it was baked as hard as rock. It was summer now . . . early afternoon . . . and the sun was yellow and hot.

Finding the saloon, Slocum saw what he was looking for. Tied to the hitching rail out front were a couple of horses that were an exact match of the description Paul had given him.

At that moment the stagecoach Slocum had seen earlier came rolling into town, its driver whistling and shouting at the team. As was often the case, the driver had urged the team into a trot at the edge of town. That way, the coach would roll in rapidly, making a somewhat more dramatic arrival than it would have had the team been walking. Glancing toward the coach, Slocum saw the face of a very pretty young woman looking back at him through the right rear window.

The coach stopped in front of the depot at the far end of the street, and a half dozen people crowded around it. Slocum turned his attention back to the task at hand and checking the pistol in his holster, he went into the saloon.

The shadows made the saloon seem cooler inside, but

that was illusory. It was nearly as hot inside as out, and without the benefit of a breath of air it was even more stifling. The customers were sweating in their drinks and wiping their faces with bandannas.

As always when he entered a strange saloon, Slocum checked the place out. To one unfamiliar with what he was doing, Slocum's glance appeared to be little more than idle curiosity. But it was a studied surveillance. Who was armed? Why type guns were they carrying? How were they wearing them? Was there anyone here he knew? More importantly, was there anyone here who knew him and who might take this opportunity to settle some old score, real or imagined, for himself or a friend?

It appeared that there were only workers and drifters here. The couple of men who were armed were young men, probably wearing their guns as much for show as anything. And from the way the pistols rode on their hips, Slocum would have bet that they had never used them for anything but target practice, and not very successfully at that.

The bartender stood behind the bar. In front of him were two glasses with whiskey remaining in them, and he poured the whiskey back into a bottle, corked it, and put the bottle on the shelf behind the bar. He wiped the glasses out with his stained apron, then set them among the unused glasses. Seeing Slocum step up to the bar, the bartender moved down toward him.

"Whiskey," Slocum said.

The barman reached for the bottle he had just poured the whiskey back into, but Slocum pointed to an unopened bottle.

"That one," he said.

Shrugging, the saloonkeeper pulled the cork from the fresh bottle.

"I'm looking for two men," Slocum said.

"Mister, if you want whiskey or beer, I'm your man. If you want anything else, I can't help you," the bartender replied.

"They were riding the horses tied up out front. One of the men is a big, sandy-haired galoot."

"I told you, mister. What I do is pour drinks. Other than that, I mind my own business."

"They are murdering scum," Slocum said. "Killed a rancher and his wife . . . raped the wife before they killed her."

"You the law?"

"No," Slocum said. "The rancher and his wife were friends of mine."

"People like that, you ought to let the law handle."

"The law had them. They were about to be hanged, but they killed the deputy and escaped."

"There a reward?"

"If there is, I'm not payin' it," Slocum said.

"What do these fellas look like?"

"One of them has one of his eyelids cut so that it's half closed all the time. The other has a flat nose and a scar on his right cheek."

The barkeeper didn't say anything, but Slocum noticed a slight reaction to his description.

"They're here right now, aren't they?" Slocum asked.

The saloon owner said nothing, but he raised his head and looked toward the stairs at the back of the room.

"Thanks," Slocum said.

At the back of the saloon, a flight of wooden stairs led up to an enclosed loft. Slocum guessed that the two doors at the head of the stairs led to the rooms used by prostitutes who worked in the saloon. Slocum started to pull his gun, then thought better of it, and slipped out his knife instead.

The few men in the saloon had been talking and laughing among themselves. When they saw Slocum pull his knife, their conversations died, and they watched him walk quietly up the steps.

From the rooms above him he could hear muffled sounds that left little doubt as to what was going on behind the closed doors. Normally such sounds called forth ribald comments from the patrons below, but now there was no teasing whatsoever; everyone knew that a life-and-death confrontation was about to take place. No one knew why, but then, such things occurred often, and no one really cared about the reasons.

Slocum tried to open the first door, but it was locked. He knocked on it.

"Go 'way, Dingo," a man's voice called from the other side of the door. "You've had your woman, now let me have mine."

"Go 'way, Dingo," he said. That meant Dingo was in the other room.

From what he had been able to determine, Dingo was the brains of the two. If he got Dingo, Flatnose would be easy pickings.

Slocum moved to the next door, raised his foot, then kicked it hard. The door flew open with a crash and the woman inside the room screamed.

"What the hell?" the man shouted. He stood up quickly, and Slocum saw with a sinking feeling that it wasn't Dingo. He heard a crash of glass from the next room and he dashed to the window and looked down. He saw Dingo just getting to his feet from the leap to the alley below.

"Damn!" He'd been suckered in by an old trick. Angus Dingo had deliberately used his own name when he said go away, in order to throw Slocum off. Slocum kicked out the window and started to climb onto the sill to go after Dingo.

"You sonofabitch! Who the hell are you?" Flatnose shouted. Out of the corner of his eye, Slocum saw Flatnose coming after him with a knife. He lunged toward Slocum, making a long, would-be, stomach-opening swipe. Slocum barely managed to avoid the point of the knife. One inch closer and he would have been disemboweled.

"I'll cut you open like a pig, you sonofabitch," Flatnose growled. "Who the hell you think you are, bustin' in like this?"

Flatnose swung again and Slocum jumped deftly to one side, then counterthrust. The blade of his knife buried itself in the man's neck, and Slocum felt hot blood spilling across his hand. The man gurgled and his eyes bulged open wide. Then, slowly, he slipped to the floor.

"Angus Dingo," Slocum said, kneeling beside the wounded man. "Where is he heading?"

"Who . . . who are you?" Flatnose asked. Blood bubbled at his lips when he spoke.

"The name is Slocum. John Slocum."

"You ain't the law?"

"No."

"I'll be damned," Flatnose gasped. "I got myself kilt for nothin'."

"Where is Angus Dingo?" Slocum asked again.

"If you ain't the law, why did you come after us?"

"Where is he?" Slocum asked, without answering Flatnose's question.

"I reckon you'll just have to keep lookin' for him," Flatnose said, dying with the laughter from hell on his lips.

Slocum stood up angrily. He had lost valuable time trying to get the outlaw to talk. He turned and ran from the room, down the stairs, and out the front. Both outlaw horses were gone. That gave Dingo an advantage, because by switching from horse to horse, he would be able to extend his range.

Slocum found the black gelding five miles later. He found the roan five miles after that, contentedly cropping grass. He also found the body of a man stripped to his underwear. The clothes Dingo had been wearing were in a pile nearby. Angus Dingo now had different clothes and a different horse.

Slocum threw the body over the back of the roan, then brought it back to Whiskey Wells with him.

"His name is Evers, Jason Evers," the marshal said, standing in front of his office, lifting the head of the body for a closer examination. "He's a drummer. Did you kill him?"

"Doesn't seem likely I would've brought him back here if I'd killed him, does it?" Slocum asked.

The marshal expectorated a wad of tobacco, then wiped his mouth with the back of his hand.

"No," he agreed. "That don't seem likely a'tall. But then, I wouldn't a figured you would come back here after killin' that flat-nosed fella either, but here you are."

Slocum moved his hand to his gun. "Marshal, you aren't trying to say . . ."

"Now, hold on there," the marshal said easily. "You ain't in no trouble. Leastwise, not with me, you ain't. The whore that was with the man you kilt told me what happened. Said the flat-nosed fella come after you with a knife. I figure that makes it self-defense."

Slocum relaxed a little.

"Who was he?" the marshal asked. "The fella you kilt."

"His name was Flatnose Nelson. The other one, the one who got away, was Angus Dingo."

"Damn, I've heard of both of 'em. Word I got was they escaped the hangman's noose some days back. And they was both in my town?"

"This is where I found them."

"Why was you lookin' for them? The whore said you wasn't the law. You a bounty hunter?"

"No."

"Then what was you after them for?"

"They killed some friends of mine," Slocum said.

"Reason enough, I reckon," the marshal replied, carving off another chew of tobacco. "I'm sorry the sonofabitch got away from you."

"He didn't."

"He didn't?"

"Not permanently," Slocum said. "I'll catch up with him one of these days."

4

John Slocum, freshly bathed, shaved, and shorn, took a table at Ma Lambert's Restaurant and began perusing the menu. He sensed someone approaching his table, but didn't look up from the menu. Instead, he started to order.

"I'll have steak, potatoes . . ."

"Have anything you want, *Monsieur* Slocum. It's all on me," a woman said. Her voice was throaty and she spoke with a definite French accent.

Slocum looked up in surprise. Standing over him was a very pretty woman, tall and slender, though rounded enough so that no one could doubt her sex, even from a distance. Her skin was olive-toned, her cheekbones high, her eyes brown, and her hair black as a raven's wing. This was, he realized, the same woman he had seen looking through the window of the stagecoach when it arrived.

"I'm sorry, I thought you were the waitress."

"Non, monsieur, je ne suis pas la serveuse."

"Yes, I can see that you aren't."

"However, it would give me great *plaisir* if you would *permettez-moi* to pay for your dinner," the woman added.

29

Slocum smiled. "Ordinarily, I'm not one to look a gift horse in the mouth. But when I get an offer like this, and from a beautiful woman, I hope you understand that I have to ask why."

"But of course I understand," the woman replied. "I would like to dine with you, *monsieur*. That would guarantee me a few moments of your time."

"Be my guest," Slocum said. "Or, under the circumstances, I suppose I am your guest."

The proprietor of the restaurant approached the table then. A soiled towel was thrown over one shoulder.

"What can I get you folks?" he asked.

"Bifteck, Pomme de terre, et un vin bon et rouge, s'il vous plaît."

The proprietor blinked at the order. "Lady, I didn't understand one word you just said, but it's a cinch I ain't got nothing like that here."

The woman laughed, and started to repeat the order when Slocum spoke up.

"She ordered steak, potatoes, and a good red wine," Slocum said. "I'm sure you have the steak and potatoes, I'm not sure about the wine."

The woman smiled across the table. "I'm impressed, *monsieur*. You speak French."

"Not really. But I've ordered a few meals in New Orleans," Slocum replied.

"Yeah, well, I got the steak and potatoes all right, but you're right about the wine," the proprietor said. "I ain't got no wine, especially nothin' fancy. Whiskey, beer, tea, or coffee."

"I'll have beer," Slocum said.

"Coffee," the woman said.

The proprietor nodded, leaned over to wipe off the table

with the towel he had across his shoulder, then disappeared into the kitchen.

"I think we should introduce ourselves," the woman said. "Or at least, I should introduce myself. I know who you are, *Monsieur* John Slocum."

"How do you know my name?"

"Oh, I know much more than your name, *monsieur*," she said. "But, we won't go into that now. My name is Danielle Garneau."

"Nice to meet you, *Mademoiselle* Garneau. Or, is it Madame?"

The woman had a lilting laugh that sounded a bit like the tinkling of wind chimes. "Why don't you just call me Danielle."

"All right. Danielle it is," Slocum said.

"Now, you asked how I know you. I have made it a point to get as much information about you as I could. I learned, not only your name, but discovered that you are a man of considerable skill in certain, uh, shall we say, critical areas. You have the reputation of being exceptionally proficient with firearms and knives."

The meal arrived then, and for a moment, Danielle quit talking. Once the proprietor had withdrawn, she resumed her discourse.

"Unlike many others who have such skills, you do not have the reputation of being a bully, and, though I have spent an enormous amount of money on telegrams in the last few days, I have been unable to find a single outstanding warrant against you."

"Why?"

"Why do you have no outstanding warrants?" Danielle asked, a puzzled expression on her face.

"No," Slocum replied. He cut a piece of steak. It was pink and bloody, exactly the way he liked it.

"Why have you gone to so much trouble to find out about me?"

"I need a job done, John." When she said his name, the "J" was soft, so that it sounded like Zhon. "It is a very dangerous job. I thought I had found the man to do the job for me, but as it turned out, he wasn't the man after all."

"He beat you out of some money?"

"In a manner of speaking, you might say that he did," Danielle replied. "Though it wasn't his fault. I'm sure he intended to fulfill the contract."

"What happened to him?" Slocum washed down a piece of steak with a swallow of beer.

"You killed him," Danielle said, easily. "His name was Kyle Bodine."

Slocum studied her over the rim of his beer glass. "He said something about hiring out his guns. He was working for you?"

"Oui, monsieur."

"Lady, I don't know what you hired him to do for you, but it's unlikely I'd be interested in anything he was willing to do."

"Oh, but you are already doing it, *monsieur*," Danielle said. "I want to hire you to find Angus Dingo and bring him to justice."

"Why are you interested in seeing Angus Dingo brought to justice?"

"Because he killed Keeta Rouchon."

"Keeta Rouchon?"

"Keeta worked for me in New Orleans, at the *Chambre du Plaisir*. The House of Pleasure," she translated for him.

"House of Pleasure? Would that be a . . ."

"Oui. It was a bordello, *monsieur,"* Danielle said. "You

don't have to be afraid of the word. I run the best bordello in New Orleans."

Slocum smiled. "If the girls who work for you are as pretty as the boss lady, I don't doubt it."

"You are too kind, *monsieur*," Danielle replied. "And you will have the opportunity to judge for yourself, as some of my girls will be joining us in the search."

Slocum had just started to take another bite of steak, but he let his hand drop quickly to the table.

"Hold on!" he said. "Joining us, did you say?"

"*Oui*. Keeta was very popular with all the girls. Like me, they want to see her killer brought to justice."

"He will be brought to justice," Slocum said. "But there is no 'us' involved in the search, so there is no 'joining us.'"

"Oh, but we must join you. That is part of the deal. I am paying you to not only search for Angus Dingo, but to act as our guide. We want to go with you, we want to take an active part in the search and capture of this man."

"You must be out of your mind to think I would even consider such a thing. Take a bunch of women with me while I search for a killer? That is the most outrageous thing I have ever heard."

"Perhaps if you would listen to my side I could persuade you to change your mind," Danielle suggested. "I can make it well worth your while."

"No. Absolutely not. Anyway, why would you want to spend the money? I told you I'm already going after him. There's no need for you to pay me to do what I am already going to do."

"I know you are going after him anyway. And I know you will find him and bring him to justice. That isn't the point."

"Then what is the point?"

"The point is, my girls and I want to participate. We want the personal satisfaction of knowing that we had a hand in finding Angus Dingo."

"No."

"*Monsieur*, would it help any, if I told you that Keeta Rouchon is the woman you knew as Kathy Caulder?"

"Kathy Caulder? Wait a minute, are you telling me that Kathy was a whore?"

"A former whore," Danielle said. "A girl who met and fell in love with someone, someone who knew about her past, but could love her all the same. Don't you understand, *Monsieur* Slocum, that this is the dream of all girls who are on the line? And if one of them makes it out she takes with her a little piece of the soul of all her friends. When Dingo killed Keeta, he destroyed that collective soul."

Slocum sighed. "I understand what you are saying, Danielle. But, what you are asking is just not possible. In fact, if I tried to take you and a dozen or so . . ."

"Only two more," Danielle said, quickly. "Marie De-Jourlet and Deliliah Breaux."

"All right, if I took three of you, the chances of finding Dingo are much, much slimmer. In fact, I might not be able to find him at all."

"With anyone else I would say that is true," Danielle said. "But you, *monsieur?* You have the experience, knowledge, and skill it would take to do such a thing. I have no doubt that you can find him, with or without our tagging along. I just prefer that it be with us. And I am prepared to pay very handsomely for that opportunity."

Slocum sighed, and drummed his fingers on the table in contemplation. Danielle had caught him at a particularly vulnerable time. He was broke.

"When you say you are willing to pay handsomely for the opportunity to come along . . . just how handsomely would that be?"

Slocum wanted to bite his tongue, to call the question back. He had no intention of taking three women with him while he trailed Dingo. So why did he even bother to ask?

"Five thousand dollars," Danielle said, without blinking an eye.

"Five thousand dollars?" Slocum repeated, asking the question so loudly that everyone else in the restaurant turned to look at him. Then more quietly, he said again, "You are willing to pay five thousand dollars for the right to come along on my search for Dingo?"

"Yes, I will pay that, plus any and all expenses we incur along the way."

"Lady," Slocum started, but Danielle held up her finger as she smiled at him.

"It is Danielle, remember?"

"Danielle," Slocum corrected. "I know I'm going to regret this. But you have just signed on to the search. When do the other girls arrive? I don't want the trail to get too cold."

"They will be here on tomorrow's stage," Danielle promised.

It was warm in the hotel room, and Slocum lay on top of the mattress with his hands folded behind his head, staring up at shadows projected on the ceiling by the silver light of a bright moon. He was already having second thoughts about the deal he had just made, agreeing to take three women with him on his hunt for Angus Dingo. On the other hand, Danielle had paid in advance, in cash, and the thought of that much money stuffed down into his saddlebag made the deal somewhat easier to accept.

He heard a light knock on the door, and, snaking the pistol from its holster he called out, "Who's there?"

Afterward, he moved quickly in case someone on the other side decided to shoot toward the sound of the voice.

"It is I, Danielle. May I come in, John?"

Without answering, Slocum stepped over to the door and unlocked it. He pulled it open while, at the same time stepping back out of the way. A pie-shaped wedge of golden light spilled into the room from the kerosene lamps that lit the hallway. Danielle stepped into the wedge of light, but didn't see Slocum.

"John?" she called in confusion. "John, are you here?"

"I'm here," Slocum said quickly, from the shadows alongside the door.

"Oh, I was afraid for a moment that . . . why are you standing in the shadows?"

"I have developed the habit of being cautious," Slocum replied.

Danielle laughed, a low, throaty laugh. "Surely John Slocum, you weren't wary of me."

"I'm wary of everyone. It helps keep me alive." He stepped out into the light then, and Danielle gasped.

"Mon Dieu! You're naked," she said. "Do you always sleep naked?"

"Not always."

Danielle had put on some perfume and Slocum could smell its note: a scent of lilac, a hint of coriander and something else; a womanly musk which came not from the perfume, but from her own excitement. Slocum felt his pulse increase and his manhood rise.

"I couldn't sleep," Danielle said. "It came to me as I was lying in bed, that we had not sealed our bargain."

"You've given me the money. What sort of seal are you talking about?" Slocum asked.

"I'm not exactly sure," Danielle said. "But, I thought I might be able to come up with an idea." Danielle let her hand trail down Slocum's stomach, across the wiry bush of hair, then to his cock, which was now standing straight up. Slowly, tentatively, she wrapped her fingers around it.

"You knew, didn't you? You knew I would come to you tonight." Quickly, Danielle slipped out of her dress. She was wearing nothing underneath.

"Let's just say that I hoped you would," Slocum said. He reached out to touch her. His fingers passed across silky smooth skin, traced a path from her shoulder to the curve of a breast, and out to a hard, little nipple. He rubbed it gently.

"Ohhh," Danielle said, shivering under his touch. "I think I'm going to like our business arrangement. Do you want to make love, John?" She asked the question as if she were offering him a cup of coffee, and she moved over to the bed to be ready for him if he answered in the affirmative.

Following her to the bed, Slocum lay beside her, then put his arms around her and pulled her close to him. Her lips came to his and he parted them with his tongue. She didn't retreat from him, but met his tongue with her own in a tangling duet of taste and texture. Danielle was a woman of experience and passion, and she responded to him like a wild animal, writhing, moaning, and flailing her hands about his body. Slocum moved his mouth from her lips and began kissing her on the neck, sucking the flesh up into his mouth and biting it.

Danielle increased the tempo of her movements, running her hands up and down his back as if looking for a handhold. Slocum pinched the lobe of her ear gently between his lips, then stuck his tongue in her ear. He saw her nipple in the soft, silver glow from the moonlight, straining as if it were trying to open. He put her breast in his mouth, then rubbed her other nipple with the tips of his fingers.

"*Oui*," Danielle said. "*Oui, oui, vous êtes très magnifique.*"

Danielle saw Slocum move from breast to breast with his mouth, then seek out the other parts of her body. She lay there, feeling her body being loved, and watching as the head of her lover moved about on her, arousing her to dizzying heights of sensation. She saw his head slide down across her stomach, then kiss her on the inside of each thigh. Her legs trembled uncontrollably. She was in ecstasy, deriving pleasure from the slightest touch, or from the brush of his lips, no matter where they were placed. She was primed in every fiber of her being for sex. Her body longed for it, her mind craved it, and she was about to get that need fulfilled.

Danielle's moans of pleasure turned into cries for release. "Oh, John, now, please, now! Don't make me wait any longer!"

Slocum felt as if his very blood had turned to boiling oil. Every inch of his body was sensitized to pleasure. He moved up and spread her legs, then came down on her, pushing his throbbing cock into the hot, wet cavern that was open to him. As he buried himself in her, he felt her hands digging into his back, dislodging pleasure and sending it through the rest of his body, until his whole being was yearning for release.

Suddenly he felt Danielle tense all over. "Oh," she said. "So quickly. Never has it happened so quickly for me!

Oh . . . oh . . . oh!" Each spasm of her climax brought the word out in little barks of pleasure as, with big sporadic jerks, she gave herself over to the release she had attained.

Slocum couldn't hold himself back any longer, and he felt himself escaping through the part of him that was joined with Danielle. For a fleeting instant, he tried to hold back, then he gave up, and with a final thrust, purged his body of the escaping energy. He could feel the extreme sensitivity of Danielle's breasts, and the completeness of the pleasure Danielle had just attained.

After a few moments, Danielle's hands began roaming again. They found Slocum, now in a flaccid state, and with a few expert strokes, soon had him erect again. This time their lovemaking was slower, and they were able to coast up to the edge of a climax, spend a moment reveling in the delightful sensations, then back away from it without going over the edge. They kept this up for a long time, with slow pleasurable strokes, exchanged kisses, and the sensitized contact of naked skin against naked skin, until, once more, they were complete.

Finally, Danielle got up and put her dress on. Leaning over the bed, she kissed Slocum on the forehead.

"I'm glad we had this night," she said. "After Marie and Delilah arrive, I won't have you to myself anymore."

She left the room, pulling the door closed gently, behind her.

Slocum thought about what lay ahead of him. If Marie and Delilah were anything like Danielle, and he was pretty sure they were, then his next several days promised to be very interesting. And exhausting, he added as an afterthought.

5

Dingo sat on his horse on top of a ridge and looked down on the little ranch before him. The house, barn, and smokehouse looked well cared-for, evidence that the ranch was well run. That also meant that there would be meat in the smokehouse, and probably an ample supply of flour, coffee, and beans, everything he would need for an extended stay on the trail.

Shortly after leaving Whiskey Wells, Dingo had run into two old acquaintances, Kelly and a half-breed. Kelly was an Irishman, red-haired, and missing a couple of front teeth. The meeting was not by chance, for it had been Kelly who broke him out of jail. The half-breed was dark and brooding, but nobody was quite sure what sort of breed he was.

Kelly was dismounted, standing over by a rock, relieving himself. The sound of splashing water had been going on for several seconds.

"You piss long time," the breed grunted.

"A man's gotta do what a man's gotta do," Kelly said. He finished, shook himself off, then buttoned up his pants.

"How long we gonna stay here?" he asked, as he climbed up into the saddle.

"Not much longer," Dingo replied. "It's nearly supper-time."

Fifteen-year-old Link Peabody held his head under the mouth of the pump while he worked the handles. Ice-cold, deep-well water cascaded over him, washing away the dirt and sweat from an afternoon of hard work in the field. He reached for the towel he had draped across the split-rail fence, but it was gone. He heard a girl's giggle.

"Louise," he said, angrily. "Gimmie back that towel you took."

"What towel?" Louise teased.

Link rubbed the water out of his eyes then opened them and saw his twin sister standing there, holding the towel behind her back. She was smiling at him.

"If you don't want me to dry my face on your dress, you'll gimme back that towel," Link growled.

"Oh, you mean *this* towel?" Louise asked. She handed the towel to him.

"Very funny." Link took the towel and began drying his face. Louise stood beside him, examining her finger-nails. Link knew his sister well enough to know that she was about to ask him for something.

"All right, what is it?" Link asked.

"What do you mean?"

"You want something. What is it? My pocketknife?"

"What would a woman want with a pocketknife?" Louise replied.

Link chuckled. "Woman? You wanted to use it yester-day. Did you become a woman in one day?"

"Link, Papa won't let me go to the church picnic with

Terry Rawlings." Louise pouted. "He says I'm too young."

"You are too young," Link said easily.

"Too young? I'm the same age as you, Lincoln Peabody."

"That don't make no difference. You're a girl. It's different with girls."

"I'm not a girl, I'm a woman, near 'bout," she said. Louise leaned against the split-rail fence and thrust her hip out, proudly displaying the developing curves of her young body. "You tell Papa to let me go to the picnic with Terry. Papa will listen to you."

"Ha! In a pig's eye, he will," Link said. He draped the towel back across the rail. "What's for supper? I'm 'bout starved."

"Breaded pork chops and fried potatoes," Louise said. "And I made 'em myself."

"They'll probably poison me," Link teased.

Brother and sister walked back up the path to the house, following the rich aroma of fried pork. Link pushed the door open, then came to a complete halt, his eyes wide with confusion.

There were three strange men in the kitchen. One was stocky and red-haired, with stitch marks over his right eyebrow. He was standing behind George, Link's father, holding a gun to his father's head. Another was a breed, swarthy, with dark, brooding eyes. The third was a big man. One of his eyelids had been cut so that it was half-closed all the time. This one was standing behind the table eating a pork chop, which he held in his left hand. Bits of grease and breading clung to his chin. Although no one in the Peabody family knew it, this was Angus Dingo.

"Well, now, would you look here at this sweet little thing?" Dingo said. "She'll do fine. Yes, sir, she'll do just real fine." He looked at Louise with eyes that shined in unabashed lust.

"Who are you?" Link asked. "What are you doing with my ma and pa?"

"Boy, you ain't needed," Dingo said. He pulled out his gun and before anyone could say a word, pulled the trigger. The gun roared as a wicked flash of flame jumped from the barrel of the gun and a cloud of smoke billowed out over the table. The bullet hit Link in the forehead, then burst out from the back of his head, carrying with it bits of bone, skin, and brain matter. Heavy drops of blood splattered from Link's wound onto Louise's face and fanned out onto the bodice of her dress.

"Link!" she screamed, as her brother, already dead, fell back, half in the house and half out on the back porch.

"Murderers!" Link's mother yelled. She tried to stand up, but one of the men shoved her back down in her chair, then cut a nick in her face with the tip of his knife. A bright red stream of blood began flowing from the cut.

"Martha!" George shouted, but his shout was cut off by a blow to the back of his head as the red-haired man brought his gun down sharply.

George Peabody opened his eyes and saw the stars of a midnight sky. For a moment he wondered where he was, and why he was sleeping outside. Then he felt the pain in his head and recalled vividly seeing his son murdered. He tried to get up, but discovered that he was tied.

"Are you all right?" Martha asked.

"What's going on?" George asked. "Where are we?"

"We're in the back of a wagon," Martha said. "They are taking us somewhere."

"Link?"

"He's . . . he's dead," Martha said.

"Louise?"

"I'm here, Papa," Louise said. George struggled to turn over and saw his daughter sitting against the side of the wagon, her knees drawn up, her arms wrapped around her legs.

"Are you hurt?"

"No."

"You're not tied," George said. He looked toward the wagon seat and saw the half-breed driving. The other two were riding just ahead of the wagon, leading the half-breed's horse.

"Louise, slip down over the back," George said. "Slip down and run away."

"No," Louise said. "Papa, they said if I tried to run away they'd kill you and Mama."

"They'll probably do that anyway," George said. "Go on, get away."

"I can't," Louise said. "Papa if I run and they kill you, I . . . I wouldn't want to live."

George struggled until he was finally able to sit up. He looked around outside the wagon, caught the gleam of moonlight on a stream of water. "That's Sage Creek," he said. "What are we doing this far from home?"

"I don't know. They've been talking very quietly. I don't know what they are planning," Martha said.

"Hey!" the half-breed called, and the two men stopped, then came back to the wagon.

"What do you want?"

"Man awake."

Dingo came back to look down into the wagon. He rubbed his cheek as he looked at his three prisoners. "Get out of the wagon, girl," he said.

"Papa?" Louis said in a quiet, frightened voice.

"Don't be goin' to your papa, girl, there ain't a damned

thing he's gonna be able to do about it but watch."

"No!" George shouted then, realizing what the men had in mind. "No, leave her alone!"

The half-breed hit George in the face with his fist. George had no way to ward off the blow, no way to dodge it. His eye puffed shut, and his head banged against the side of the wagon.

"The girl's mine," Dingo said.

"Well, hell, you're gonna share with us, ain't you?" Kelly asked.

"Yeah," Dingo said. "Yeah, I'm gonna share with you. Soon's I'm finished with her, you can have all you want."

"Please," Martha begged. "Please, leave her alone. If you must do something . . . take me."

Dingo laughed. "Oh, you'd like that, wouldn't you, woman?" He rubbed himself. "I spec you'd like that a lot, getting yourself some real men 'stead o' that farmer you're married to. But, we ain't interested in you. We want somethin' young, somethin' pretty."

"No . . . please, no," Martha begged.

"Woman, you jus' gonna have to take your pleasure from watchin'," Dingo said in a low, gravelly voice. Then, smiling evilly at the girl, he grabbed himself. "Look what I got for you."

George yelled his defiance at them, and Dingo, afraid that someone might be passing by, nodded at the half-breed to hit him again. This time George went out from the blow. When he regained consciousness a while later, he saw Louise lying on the ground naked, her legs spread wide. He looked over at his wife. She, too, was naked and her body was covered with cuts and welts, evidence of the torture she had undergone while George was unconscious.

Dingo, apparently just finished, was buckling his pants

as he stood over Louis's prostrate form. He rubbed the back of his hand across his mouth.

"Well, now, I got 'er all broke in for you. Who's gonna be next?"

"My God! You . . . you raped her!" George said, realizing what happened while he was out.

"Naw, it warn't rape. Jus' a little friendly lovin', that's all."

The half-breed grunted something, then dropped his trousers to his ankles and came down over the young girl.

"No! No!" George shouted.

"Put a gag on him," Dingo said. "The woman, too. We can't keep knockin' him out to keep 'im quiet. 'Sides, I want him to watch."

Louise lay unmoving beneath the half-breed. Her eyes were open but they had a glazed-over, blank look, as if her soul had died. She didn't make one sound as the half-breed grunted out his evil pleasure on her.

Marie and Delilah were as pretty as Danielle. Marie was red-haired; Deliliah's hair was the color of ripe wheat. Shortly after they arrived, Danielle gave Slocum money and asked him to buy the horses and whatever other equipment they would need for the journey. He bought three horses, riding each of them first to test them as being suitable mounts for the women. All three passed the test.

Slocum also bought clothes for the women, buying them denim trousers and cotton shirts. They would balk at the idea of wearing men's clothes, but it just might keep them alive. Four men riding together were much more formidable, and much less attractive as a target, than would be one man and three women.

To Slocum's surprise, the women didn't complain at

all. On the contrary, they seemed to take a rather strange delight in dressing as men.

"Let's face it, ladies," Delilah said to the other two women. "Men's clothes are a lot more practical than women's clothes. I'll bet you there will come a time when ladies can wear pants and a shirt as easily as men."

Delilah was the shortest of the three women, and definitely the most shapely. Whereas the other two might pass as men in a cursory examination, no one seeing Delilah's curvy body would mistake her.

"Let's face it, Delilah," Marie said, mimicking Delilah. "Ladies we ain't."

All three women laughed, and Slocum shook his head. The banter was light, spirited, and very animated. It turned out that, despite the French-sounding names, only Danielle was actually French, and she wasn't really French, she was Creole. Delilah and Marie were strictly Midwestern girls who had taken French names.

"When you work in a French whorehouse, the men think you should be French," Delilah explained.

"And we always do what the men want," Marie said, then she added, *"Monsieur."*

"We can show you, if you want," Delilah said, putting her fingers to Slocum's cheek then stroking it lightly.

"Girls, there is no time for that now," Danielle said. *"Monsieur* Slocum is anxious to begin the hunt. And I am, too."

"All right," Delilah said, pulling her hand away. "I'm sure we'll find time . . . later."

"Any instructions before we leave, John?" Danielle asked.

"Yes," Slocum said. "Wear no face paint, pile your hair up under your hats, and say nothing that might give you away by the sound of your voice. Have you got that?"

"Oui, monsieur," Danielle replied.

Half an hour later the three women, dressed as Slocum had instructed them, came out of the hotel, mounted their horses, and rode out of town. The town took little notice of them as they left. That was exactly the way Slocum wanted it.

6

Slocum and the three women came across the Peabody ranch at midmorning.

"John," Danielle said. "Could we stop at that ranch for a few minutes? They have a privy."

"Yes," both Marie and Delilah added.

"I thought you weren't going to ask for any special privileges," Slocum teased.

"Well, after all, we can't stand up and pee against a tree like you can," Delilah said. "It hardly seems a special privilege to want to use a privy when the opportunity presents itself."

"Ahh, I was just teasing you," Slocum said. "Go ahead, it'll give me a chance to water the horses. Also, they may have seen something that could be helpful. We'll stop in for a few minutes."

Slocum turned his horse toward the ranch and the three women followed.

When they arrived and tied their horses off at the hitching rail, they could hear the cow bawling in the barn.

"What's that?" Danielle asked.

"Sounds like a cow that needs milking," Marie said. "Sort of late for it not to have been milked."

Slocum chuckled. "You know about milking cows, do you?"

"I wasn't born in a whorehouse," Marie replied.

"You're right, though, it does seem a little late for the cow not to have been milked," Slocum said. He cupped his hands around his mouth. "Hello the house! Anyone home?"

"John, I don't like this. This is kind of spooky," Delilah said. "Let's go."

"Without using the privy?" Slocum asked.

"We can find a bush somewhere."

The cow bawled again, and Slocum looked toward the barn. "I don't know who lives here," he said. "But it looks like they keep the place up really well. And anyone who keeps a place up this well, wouldn't let a cow go this long without being milked." He started toward the back.

"Where are you going?" Danielle asked.

"Something's not right here. I'm going to have a look around."

When Slocum reached the back corner of the house he heard the sound of a hundred or more buzzing flies. The sound stopped him cold. He had heard buzzing flies before and he knew when they buzzed with this kind of intensity, there was a reason. The first time he had heard flies like this was at Shiloh. On the evening of the first day of the big battle, hundreds of bodies were left lying on the battlefield. When Slocum looked at the bodies from a distance, they were black and moving from the thousands of flies that were drawn to the feast. The flies made the same sound then as he was hearing now.

Slocum drew his gun, then began to creep very slowly around the corner of the house. The back door to the house was standing open and lying half out of the back door, with his head on the back porch, was a young boy, no older than fifteen or sixteen. His eyes were open and there was a hole in his forehead, with a bigger hole in the back of his head. This was what had drawn all the flies.

Slocum stepped up to the door and looked into the house. He saw the table set for a meal. There were pork chop bones on the tablecloth and scattered about on the floor. The meal had been eaten, but not from the plates, which were still clean and in their place. Cautiously, he began looking through the house. There was not one trace of another human being.

When Slocum walked back to the front of the house the three women were standing in a quiet group. Although they hadn't gone around back to see what was there, they were intuitive enough to know that something was, and they looked at Slocum with anxious expressions on their faces.

"What did you find, John?" Danielle asked.

"A young boy," Slocum said. "He's been shot."

"Dead?"

Slocum nodded. "No one else is here."

"What are we going to do?"

Slocum nodded toward a nearby sycamore tree, under which there were a couple of tombstones. "Looks like that might be the family burial plot over there," he said. "I'm going to go dig a grave. Marie, you milk the cow. Danielle, you and Delilah see if you can find something to use as a shroud, then get the boy in it. I'll bury him."

Marie started toward the barn, but Danielle and Delilah hesitated for a moment.

"What is it?" Slocum asked. "What's wrong?"

"The boy," Danielle said. "Is it . . . awful?"

Slocum sighed. "I won't lie to you. Yes, it is. But you

wanted to come, all three of you. More than likely you are going to see much worse than this before it's all over. It might even be one of the three of you."

The women flinched at the thought.

"I told you what you were getting in to."

"You are right," Danielle said. "Come, Delilah. We'll find a shroud for the boy."

Half an hour later the cow was milked, the boy's body was wrapped in a canvas shroud, and lying in the bottom of the grave Slocum had dug. Slocum and the three women were standing alongside the open grave.

"Any of you know any words?" Slocum asked.

"Oui," Danielle said. "But to hear such words coming from the lips of a whore? I fear the Lord would find them blasphemous."

"I'm not much on religion," Slocum said. "But seems to me like any words that are truly spoken would be good enough, no matter whose lips they come from."

"He's right, Danielle. Say the words," Marie said.

"I'll do what I can," Danielle said, bowing her head.

It was just after noon when they saw the wagon. Slocum held out his hand, ordering the women to stay back. Then he rode quickly toward it, keeping his eyes open and his ears alert. As he approached, he saw that there were two people in the back. At first he thought they were sleeping, but when he got closer he saw that they were tightly bound. He also realized that the woman was totally naked.

He urged his horse into a gallop for the last several yards, then he jumped down to check them. They were both alive. He began untying them, first the man, then the woman. Seeing the woman's dress nearby, he spread it across her nude body in an attempt to restore some modesty. The man groaned, and Slocum got his canteen, then offered the man some water.

"Louise," the man said. "Where's Louise?"

"Your wife is here," Slocum said.

"No, my daughter. Where is my daughter?"

"I don't know. I'll look around," Slocum said.

Jumping down from the wagon, Slocum looked around the area, not expecting to find anything. To his surprise, he saw the girl, lying over in some tall grass. The girl was young, about the same age as the boy he had found earlier. She, too, was naked, and Slocum feared she might be dead, but when he hurried over to her, he saw that not only was she alive, she was conscious.

"Are you all right?" Slocum asked. It was a foolish question, he knew, but he didn't know what else to say to her. The girl was staring straight up, humming a little tune. The dark bruises on her legs and thighs provided graphic evidence as to what had happened to her.

Slocum found her dress nearby as well, and he brought it to her.

"You might want to put this on," he suggested.

The girl interrupted her humming and looked at him, though her eyes seemed to take little notice of him. After a moment she looked away and began humming the little tune again.

Slocum walked back to the wagon where the man sat, cradling his wife's head in his lap. One of the man's eyes was completely closed, his lip was puffed out, and there was blood on his face and in his hair.

Slocum whistled, then signaled for Danielle and the other two women to come to the wagon. He looked back at the man.

"Who are you, mister?" he asked.

"The name is Peabody. George Peabody. This is my

wife, Martha. Louise! Did you find her? Did you find my daughter?"

"Yes, she's over there."

"Is she . . . is she . . . ?"

"She's alive and unhurt," Slocum said.

Unhurt, Slocum thought. What a lie that was. The young girl was badly hurt, only it wasn't the kind of hurt that could be seen.

"Thank God for that."

"Who did this?"

George shook his head. "I don't know," he said. "There were three of them. I never saw them before."

"What did they look like?"

"One was redheaded, a big, heavyset man, missing a couple of teeth in front. The other one was a half-breed, wears his hair long. He's the brooding sort, don't say much. But the worst of the lot is the leader of the bunch. He's got himself a funny-looking eye."

"One of his eyes looks like it's half-closed all the time?" Slocum asked.

"Yes."

"That would be Angus Dingo," Slocum said.

"You know him?" George asked.

"I know him," Slocum said.

"If he's a friend of yours, mister, I don't care much for your friends."

"Believe me, he's no friend of mine," Slocum said. "Did you hear him called by name?"

"No. Didn't hear any names at all."

"That's all right. The way you described them, I'll recognize them if I see them. That's a big help."

"You the law?"

"No," Slocum said. "But if I catch up with them, they are going to wish I was the law."

At that moment Danielle, Marie, and Delilah arrived. Seeing three riders come up, George reacted with a start, but Slocum put his hand out, reassuringly.

"It's all right," he said. "They are with me." He looked over at Danielle. "Danielle, there's a young girl in the grass over there. Get her dressed. Marie, you and Delilah take care of Mrs. Peabody."

Without a word of dissent, the three women went about the tasks Slocum gave them.

"How did you run across these men?" Slocum asked.

"We didn't run across them. We were in our own house. The three men came in while Louise and Link were outside. I heard the door and thought it was the kids. When I looked up three men were standing there, holding guns on us. They held Martha and me in our chairs until the kids came in from washing up for supper. Then they shot Link and knocked me out. When I came to, I was tied up in the back of the wagon. They brought us here, then they took Louise out and they . . . they . . ."

"You don't have to say," Slocum said.

"They made us watch," George sobbed. "The dirty bastards made us watch!"

Danielle came walking back to the wagon then. Her arm was around the young girl, who was walking alongside her.

"Why are these women dressed like men?" George asked.

"They are with me," Slocum said, as if that were all the explanation needed.

"Oh."

"Your team looks all right," Slocum said. "Do you feel up to driving back to your house?"

"Yeah, I suppose so," George said. "Link is back there. After everything his mother and sister have been through,

I hate for them to go back and see him like that."

"They won't see him," Slocum said easily. "I didn't think he should be left out like that, so we put him in a canvas shroud and buried him out under the sycamore tree. I saw two other tombstones there. Danielle said some words over him."

"Those stones you saw are where Martha's parents are buried. I reckon Link will be with his grandparents now. I'll get a tombstone put up, and we'll hold his funeral. I appreciate it that you already said some words, but I reckon we'll need to give him a proper funeral ourselves."

"Did you happen to hear any of the men say anything that might give you a hint of where they were going?"

"No, sorry," George said.

"That's all right, I'll find them. And your description of them will help. Thanks."

"No, I thank you. If you hadn't come along when you did, I don't know what would've happened."

"You would've come to, gotten your wife and daughter dressed, and gone back home," Slocum said. "I haven't really done that much for you."

"You're going after the men who did this?"

"Yes."

"I appreciate that," George said. "But I have the feeling you would have been going after them whether this had happened or not."

"I was going after one of them, anyway. Angus Dingo," Slocum said. "I didn't know about the other two until you told me, and I thank you for the information."

"You seem to be a determined man. I don't think I would want to be in Dingo's shoes right now. What's your name, anyway?"

"Slocum," Slocum said.

The man's eyes opened a little wider. "Slocum? That would be John Slocum, would it?"

"That's right."

"Now, I'm damn sure glad I'm not in Dingo's shoes. I'd wish you luck, John Slocum, but I don't think there's any need to. From what I've heard of you, mister, you pretty much get done what you set out to do."

By now, Martha and Louise were both dressed, and sitting on the wagon seat. Martha had her arm around her daughter, who still had not acknowledged anyone, and was staring off into space, humming a little song.

"Are you going to be all right?" Slocum asked.

"Yeah, thanks to you, I am," George replied.

"Take it easy on the way back," Slocum said, handing the reins to George as he climbed onto the seat.

"Yes, sir, I will," George said. He snapped the reins against the back of the team and the two draft horses started forward immediately, relieved that after several hours of standing still, they were able to move again.

Slocum and the women remounted, then sitting astride their horses, watched the wagon as it headed back in the direction from which they had just come.

"That poor young girl," Danielle said. "Oh, I do hope she pulls through this all right."

"She will," Slocum said. "All of the people who live out here are of strong stock. The weak ones have all died out."

Turning his horse in the opposite direction of that taken by the wagon, he urged it ahead, riding toward the west. The three women followed.

7

Clouds had been building up all day and by late afternoon the rain started. There was nothing Slocum and the women could do but break out their slickers and hunker down in the saddle. Thus, when the little town of Puxico rose from the prairie in front of them, it was a welcome sight.

There was a banner spread across the street as they entered town.

CATTLEMEN'S DAY FAIR, AUG 4, 5, 6. RACES, WRESTLING, PATRIOTIC SPEECHES.

One corner of the banner had come loose and the banner was furled like a flume so that a solid gush of water poured from the end.

The first thing Slocum did after they reached town was go to the livery to get the horses out of the weather. After that, Danielle and the other girls went two doors down to the hotel where she took two rooms, one that the three women would share, and one room for Slocum.

Slocum promised to meet them for dinner in the town's only café, but first he planned to see what he could find

58

out at the saloon. Picking his way across the muddy, horesapple-strewn street, he headed toward the Brown Dirt Saloon.

A long board of wooden pegs was nailed along one wall of the saloon, about six feet from the floor. Slocum dumped the water from the crown of his hat, then hung his slicker on one of the pegs to let it drip-dry. A careful scrutiny of the saloon disclosed a card game in progress near the back. At one of the front tables, there was some earnest conversation. Three men stood at the bar, each complete within themselves, concentrating only on his drink and private thoughts. A soiled dove, near the end of her professional effectiveness, overweight, with bad teeth and wild, unkempt hair, stood at the far end. She smiled at Slocum, but getting no encouragement, stayed put.

"What'll it be, mister?" the bartender asked, making a swipe across the bar with a sour-smelling cloth.

"Whiskey, then a beer," Slocum said. He figured to drink the whiskey to warm him from the chill of the rain, then drink the beer for his thirst. The rain, as always, caused some pain in one or more of the many wounds he had sustained over his life, and though he had had every wound tended to, he was convinced that a little bit of each missile had remained behind so that the cumulative effect was nearly that of an entire bullet still lodged in his body.

The whiskey was set before him and he raised it to his lips, then tossed it down. He could feel its raw burn all the way to his stomach. When the beer was served he picked it up, then turned his back to the bar for a more leisurely survey of the room. He listened in on the conversation.

". . . what I he'erd was they was three of 'em," one of the men said. "One of 'em was a half-breed, and they come out to Miner Cobb's place and took three or four smoked hams, some beans, flour, and a side of bacon. They damn near cleaned him out without so much as a by-your-leave."

"They didn't pay him anything?"

"Not one red cent. Miner said they was that fierce lookin' enough that he figured he was lucky to get out of it alive."

"Could be them was the same three that took a couple of horses from over to the Haven farm," another said. "Didn't hear nothin' 'bout no breed, but one of 'em had an eye they said was half shut, liken as if it had been cut up pretty bad or somethin'."

Slocum walked over to the table and pointed to an empty chair. "I just rode down from Boulder," he said. "Thought maybe I'd join in with the jawboning if you folks don't mind a stranger."

"Sure thing, mister, have a seat," one of the men invited. A good talk session was more entertaining than a card game, and when a stranger from another town offered to join in, it opened up new stories and news from other places.

"Up Boulder way, huh? Would you be knowin' Andrew Dobbs?"

"Sure, I know him."

"What do you know about him?"

Slocum knew he was being tested, but he knew also that he had heard that name. He thought hard, then remembered the horseshoe-pitching contest he had ridden by when he first arrived in Boulder.

Slocum smiled. "I know that he's a pretty good barber, but not very good at horseshoes."

"Haw!" the questioner said. "Ole' Dobbs is just the

champion, that's all." He told the others so they would appreciate John's joke.

"What about a fella by the name of Bodine? Kyle Bodine? Do you know him?"

John studied the man's face. Was this also a test?

"I knew him," Slocum said. "He got himself killed." He did not volunteer the fact that he was the one who had killed him.

"Killed?" one of the others said. "I don't believe it. He's too good with a gun."

"No, the stranger's right," the one who had questioned Slocum said. "Bodine did get hisself killed."

"Well, whoever did it would have to be awful damn good."

"He was good. It was John Slocum," the man said.

"Did you see it?" Slocum asked.

"No, but I heard about it."

"Was Bodine a friend of yours?" Slocum asked.

"Mister, if you knew Kyle Bodine like you say you did, you know that he wasn't the friend of nobody. I doubt very much they was any tears shed when he got hisself shot. My name's Greg. This here fella is Paul, and that's Toby."

"I'm John," Slocum said. He leaned back in his chair and nodded a greeting while the men looked him over. They didn't see anything out of the ordinary about the stranger in their midst. He was wearing a gun and a couple of the men surmised that he probably knew how to use it. They didn't have anything to base that observation on, other than the fact that there was a look of danger about him.

"I overheard you talking about some men raiding spreads around here," Slocum said. "Maybe you'd like a bit of news I picked up."

"About these three men?"

"Could be," Slocum answered. "You did say one of them was a half-breed, didn't you?"

"Yeah, he wears his hair in long braids, like an Injun, though he might be Mexican."

"And another has a cut and a drooping eyelid?"

"Yeah, that what I hear," Greg said.

"Well, that pretty much ties up with what I've heard," Slocum said. "If it's the same three, and I believe they are, the third one of those galoots is a stocky, red-haired Irishman, with a scar on his face."

"They been over Boulder way?"

"Not exactly," Slocum replied. "But the story came to us over there, about something that happened pretty close to Whiskey Wells. Seems these three men raided the Peabody ranch, killed the boy, then raped the mother and daughter while they made Peabody watch."

"Wait a minute," Toby said. "Would this be George Peabody you're talkin' about?"

"Yes," Slocum answered. "Do you know him?"

"Hell, yes, I know him. He's a good man. About as good a man as they is. He sure set a big store in that boy of his. You say he was killed? And the woman and the girl was raped?"

"Yeah," Slocum said.

"That there's about as awful a thing as I ever heard of," Paul said. "And I've heard of some awful things."

"Well, what's the law gonna do about it?" Greg asked.

"Try an' catch 'em, I reckon," Slocum answered. "Don't know if they can. People like that move around pretty much, hard to keep up with where they're headed."

Greg scratched his chin and squinted his eyes. "Say, you know who might know somethin' about them three?" he asked.

"Who?"

"Percy. Percy Keith."

"Percy Keith?" Slocum asked. "A man about my size, has a scar on this cheek?"

"Yeah, that's him. You know him?"

"I haven't seen him in quite a while," Slocum said. "But, yes, I know him."

"Was he a drunk when you know'd him?"

"A drunk? No. No, he wasn't."

"Well he is now. Your friend is drunk near 'bout all the time," Paul said.

"I said I knew him," Slocum replied. "I didn't say we were friends."

Slocum recalled the last time he had seen Percy Keith. It had been a few years ago. Percy was riding the outlaw trail then. Their encounter was brief, but memorable enough that Slocum hadn't forgotten him.

"Well, folks say there was a time when Percy Keith was a pretty fearsome outlaw. He rode with some pretty rough people in his day. Is that true?"

"He wasn't someone you wanted on the other side of an argument," Slocum said.

"Well, he sure ain't that way now. But Greg's right. Could be Percy knows something."

"Where is he now?" Slocum asked. "I'd like to talk to him."

"First thing you do is look around at all the spittoons, make sure he ain't passed out with his head down in one of 'em," Toby said, and they all laughed.

"What you want him for, anyway?" Paul asked.

"I was just thinking that if he had any idea about where these three galoots might be headed, it might help the law find them."

"Yeah," Greg said. "Yeah, you got a point there, John."

Greg looked over toward the bar. "Hey, Billy," he yelled at the bartender. "You seen Percy around?"

"I've got 'im in the back room, stackin' crates for me," Billy answered.

"Get 'im out here. We wanna talk to 'im."

"Yeah," Toby added. "Tell 'im we'll buy him a drink. That'll bring him out."

Billy held up his finger, then walked over to the door and stuck his head into the room.

"Percy, get out here. Some fellas want to buy you a drink," he called.

A moment later a small, dispirited man came out of the room.

"Where?" he asked, anxiously.

Billy pointed to the table where Slocum and the others were sitting, and Percy shuffled over toward them, unabashedly scratching his crotch as he did so. Slocum had rarely seen a man who had come down as far as Percy had, since the last time he saw him. Percy needed a shave, and his clothes reeked of stale whiskey and sour vomit. He studied the men around the table, then stopped when he saw Slocum. Slocum could see the struggle for recollection going on in Percy's eyes. Percy raised his hand to his chin. His hand was trembling badly, though, whether from fright or the need of alcohol, Slocum couldn't tell. He pointed at Slocum with a shaking finger.

"Do I know you?" he asked. "Who are you?"

"I'm the man who's going to buy you a drink," Slocum answered.

"What . . . what do I have to do for it?"

"Just give us a little information," Greg said. "That's all."

"Information? I don't know anything about anything," Percy said quietly.

"I understand you've rode with some pretty desperate men in your day," Greg said. "Is that right?"

"I reckon I have," Percy replied.

"Who've you rode with?"

"I started out with Quantrill," Percy said. "Rode with the Reno brothers some, then took up with the James boys. Rode with Dick Liddil some, too." He reached toward the table with a shaking hand. "Can I have my drink now?"

"Not yet," Slocum said, reaching out to stop his hand. "What about Angus Dingo? You ever ride with him? He's got himself a cut eyelid that droops all the time. Right now there are two other men riding with him. One of them is a stocky, red-haired Irishman missing a couple of front teeth. The other is a half-breed, could be half-Mexican or maybe half-Indian, I'm not sure which."

There was something about the way Slocum asked his question, clearly, concisely, and demandingly, that made the others around the table look at him. Slocum ignored their glances, but stared directly into Percy's face. He saw Percy blanch. The drunk's eyes clouded over with what could only be described as fear. He took a step back from the table.

"No," Percy mumbled. "No, I never rode with anyone called Dingo. I never heard of nobody like that."

"You're lying, Percy," Slocum said matter-of-factly.

"Well, now, hold on there, mister," Greg said. "You got no call to tell a man he's lyin', just 'cause he's a drunk."

"Yeah, what makes you so sure he's lyin'?" Paul asked.

"Look at him," Slocum said. "He wants a drink bad enough to make up an answer for us, and if he didn't know, that's exactly what he would do. He does know, but right now he's more scared than thirsty. And for a man with a thirst that powerful, it's going to take a lot to frighten him away from a drink. What are you afraid of, Percy?"

"Nothin'," Percy said. "I don't know who you are talking about, that's all."

"You know, I believe John's right," Greg said. "Percy is scared. You do know this Dingo fella, don't you Percy?"

"Don't be scared," Paul said. "We're here."

"You're here?" Percy said. He tried to laugh, but it came out as a weak bark. "So, you're gonna protect me if they come for me?" For a moment, and a moment only, Percy showed a flash of his old self. "There's not one among you who wouldn't pee in his pants if you suddenly came face to face with Angus Dingo." He looked at Slocum. "Except, maybe . . ." He didn't finish his statement.

"What happened to you, Percy? When did you turn into a drunk?"

Percy stared at Slocum's face, studying it, trying hard to make the connection in his whiskey-soaked brain.

"I do know you, don't I?" Percy said.

Slocum nodded affirmatively.

"Who are you?" Percy asked.

"What about Dingo and the half-breed? You know them, too, don't you?" Slocum asked.

"What if I do?"

"Tell us," Toby said. "Tell us, so we can tell the law. My God, man, have you heard what those bastards did? They killed a fifteen-year-old boy, then they raped his mama and sister while the daddy was forced to watch. Bastards like that don't deserve to live."

"Yeah, well, when they hang, I'll stand in the crowd and watch. But I'm not gonna do anything to help the law catch them."

Greg slid a bottle of whiskey toward him. "Forget about the drink, Percy. We'll give you the whole bottle."

"Not for a bottle, not even for a case of whiskey will I tell. What good is whiskey to a dead man?"

"Percy," Slocum said quietly. "Seems to me like you're scared of the wrong people. The three men we're asking about are out there, somewhere. I'm right here in front of you. If you're going to be afraid of someone, be afraid of me."

"Yeah," Toby said laughing. "Be scared of . . ." The laughter died in his throat when he saw the expression on Slocum's face. It wasn't one of passion, or even cold fury. He wasn't sure what he saw . . . maybe something in Slocum's eyes. But he felt the hackles stand up on the back of his neck as he realized he was looking into the face of death. "My god, he means it," Toby said quietly.

"I know you, mister. I know you." Percy's words were barely audible. "I just can't call up your name."

"Sure you can."

"Son of bitch," Percy said. "Yeah, I remember now. You're John Slocum."

The name wasn't spoken very loudly, but it stopped everyone in the room as if there had been a gunshot. The card game came to a halt, the three men at the bar turned around, Billy stopped polishing glasses, and there was a deadly silence in the room.

The clock ticked loudly.

Percy's bottom lip began trembling and a line of spittle ran down his chin.

Slocum smiled. "I knew you could come up with it if you tried hard enough."

"By god. I know'd it. I know'd it was you," Percy said.

"Now, I'm going to ask you again, Percy. And I want you to think about it. And while you're thinking, I want you to know that I'm here, and they aren't."

"I . . . I know'd it was you," Percy said again, pointing at Slocum with a trembling finger. "The moment I seen you, I know'd I'd seen you afore, some'eres."

"Start talking, Percy," Slocum demanded.

Percy drew a deep breath and held his hands up. "All right, all right, I'll admit it, I've rode with Dingo before. But I didn't have nothin' to do with killin' that young boy, or rapin' that girl. Not them, not any. I've done my share of killin', but it warn't never nothin' like that."

"You rode the outlaw trail, Percy, but from what I remember of you, you never would have done anything like that. And I know you didn't have anything to do with what happened at the Peabody ranch," Slocum said. "If you did, I would've already killed you by now."

"Just so's you know," Percy said.

"Where can I find them?"

"Why you lookin' for them? You ain't the law, are you?"

"No. This is personal."

"You got any money?"

"Why?"

"If I give you any information, I'm going to need enough money to get out of here. My life won't be worth a plugged nickel if they find out I set you on them."

"How can I find them?"

Percy poured himself a glass of whiskey before he spoke again, and this time no one attempted to stop him. He drank it, then wiped the back of his hand across his mouth. "I can't tell you where to find 'em, 'cause I don't know. I could tell you the names of the other two, if that'll be any help to you."

"It'll help some," Slocum said.

"It's goin' to cost you fifty dollars."

Slocum pulled fifty dollars from his pocket and handed it over. "All right. Here's you money. Now, start talking."

"Do you know Dingo?" Percy asked, taking the money and stuffing it down into his pocket. "I mean, do you really know him?"

"No."

"Well, he's real crazy," Percy said. "He'll kill just for the hell of it. He likes killin'. And the other two is just as bad. The red-haired one you was talkin' about is Kelly O'Riley. He's a wild Irishman, used to be in the army, but he killed his sergeant, then deserted some time ago. He used to carry a dried-out tit with him that he cut off the squaw of a Sioux chief. He lost it in a poker game and has been promising to replace it with a tit from a white woman.

"The half-breed's name is Pablo Goxando. They say he killed his first man when he was fifteen. They's been others that's killed for the first time when they was only fifteen, but the man Pablo killed was his own pa. Them three is as mean a bunch as you've ever run across, or ever will. If you're goin' after them, I hope you got someone with you."

"I have three with me," Slocum said, not bothering to mention that the three with him were women. "We'll find them, all right. Knowing the names of the other two helps. Thanks, Percy."

Percy took another drink of whiskey. The whiskey had a somewhat calming effect, and he put the bottle down, this time without the shakes.

"Don't be thanking me, Slocum," he said. "If you run into them boys you might find out you've bit off more than even you can chew."

"I'll take my chances," Slocum said.

•   •   •

The rain that had started during the day continued into the night. In the distance, lightning flashed and thunder roared and the rain beat down heavily upon the roof of the hotel, then cascaded down off the eaves before drumming onto the porch overhang, below.

Slocum stood at the window of his hotel room, looking down on the street of the town. There were few people outside, and when someone did go outside he would dart quickly through the rain until he found a welcome door to slip through. The town was dark, the rain having extinguished all outside lamps, and those that were inside provided only the dullest glimmers in the shroud of night.

The room behind Slocum glowed with a soft, golden light, for he had lit the lantern and it was burning very low. Though Slocum was used to the outdoors, and had spent many a night sleeping on the prairie in such conditions, this was one of those nights where he appreciated being under a roof.

There was a quiet, almost hesitant knock at his door, and though force of habit made him pull his gun from its holster before he went to the door, he wasn't surprised to see a woman standing there. He knew one of them would be coming to him tonight, the only question had been which one it would be.

"We flipped a coin," Delilah said, as she began taking off her clothes. "And I won."

"Didn't any of you think I might have a say in this?" Slocum asked.

"The question never came up," Delilah answered with a smile. "Besides, there are three of us in that room. Only one of you in here. Are you saying you don't want to share?"

Slocum returned the smile. "I'll share," he said. He began taking off his clothes as well, doing it quickly, and without the sense of teasing seduction that Delilah was using in her own disrobing.

"Oh," Delilah said when Slocum was completely nude. "Danielle was right."

"Danielle?"

"She told us you were a magnificent speciman of a man." Delilah laughed. "Well, what she actually said was, you were a *speciman magnifiques d'un homme*." Delilah's French accent was surprisingly good.

"You're pretty good," Slocum said, referring to the accent.

"Honey, you don't know how good I really am," Delilah said. Stepping toward him, she pushed him down on the bed, then shoved her breast into his mouth.

Slocum sucked on the breast, feeling the resilience of the soft, smooth, warm flesh, then the hard, tight nipple. He ran his tongue around the nipple, while at the same time letting his hands explore her body. Delilah moaned in pleasure.

Slocum's hands moved across her flat stomach, and out along the flare of her hips, then across her thighs until they were at her warm, moist cleft. His fingers moved into the gash, slipped through the hot cream of her juices until they found the quivering little nub of flesh that sent Delilah's body into convulsive chills of pleasure.

Delilah's own hands were exploring Slocum's body as well, and he felt the delicate brush of her fingers as she touched and explored. Finally her hand wrapped around his penis, and she stroked it a few times.

Groaning from excitement, Delilah lay back on the bed and pulled Slocum onto her, while at the same time raising her legs up and guiding his cock into the damp, yielding flesh of her sex.

"Oh, sometimes it is good for me," Delilah said. "But it is never this good. I am on fire inside. Are you on fire?"

"Yes," Slocum said, and though he had answered just to satisfy her, he realized that he was. Although Danielle and Marie were in a room just down the hall, and indeed there were other patrons in the hotel, all others, and everything else, was out of his mind. For this moment all time was suspended. There was only Delilah, and nothing else existed or mattered. There was no Dingo, there was no self-imposed mission to find him. There had never been a Danielle, or any other woman, there were just the two of them, alone, in the world.

Slocum didn't realize it, but it was this singleness of purpose, this ability to make love to the woman he was with in such a way that made her realize all else had been set aside, that made him such a good lover. Every other man Delilah had ever been with—and in her profession there were many—had all been on a quest for their own pleasure. Slocum wasn't like that. He helped the woman seek her own pleasure, knowing that his would follow.

Slocum pushed deep into Delilah, feeling the rush of wet heat against his shaft. Then he began working with her, moving in and out with long, sensory-laden strokes. It was not until she had experienced several moments of intense pleasure that Delilah shuddered with her first climax.

Slocum thrust very deeply, several more times, until his own juices suddenly boiled over and shot out, spraying his pleasure deep inside Delilah. For a moment he was melting inside, pouring himself into the girl from the very marrow of his bones. Then, finally, he was through, and as the last spasm of pleasure washed through his own body, he felt the tiny quivers of aftershock, which Delilah was still enjoying. He stayed on top of her for a moment longer, then he rolled off to lie in the bed beside her, as she snuggled against him.

It wasn't until then that he realized she intended to spend the night with him. He wondered, with a satiated smile, how much sleep he would get this night.

8

The town of Brimstone, Wyoming, could not be found on any map. And whereas, most towns would resent that omission, the residents of Brimstone did not take exception to it. In fact, they went to great lengths to see to it that their town wasn't put on any maps, for they valued their privacy. Brimstone was a town founded, and occupied by, outlaws.

As Percy Keith rode into the town of Brimstone, he glanced over toward the town marshal's office. The front door was sealed shut by a couple of one-by-eight boards that were nailed across the opening in a large "X." The boards weren't substantial enough to actually keep anyone out of the building, nor were they intended to be. There had never been a town marshal's office in Brimstone, and probably never would be. The structure had been built, then symbolically closed to show that Brimstone was a town without law, except that provided by the lawless.

There were few people on the street, and those who were, moved quickly and with purpose. No one lingered for conversation. Percy headed toward the saloon at the far end of town. He had started the ride with two bottles of whiskey, bought from the money Slocum had given him. The money was supposed to enable him to get away from Dingo and the others but, the more he thought about it, the more frightened he became. He decided his best bet might be to go to Dingo and tell him that Slocum was looking for him. It might even be worth some money.

The last idea came to Percy midway through his second bottle of whiskey, and the more he thought about it, the better the idea had seemed. He didn't know for certain that Dingo would be in Brimstone, but he figured it was more likely that he would be here than anywhere else. Now, however, with the whiskey gone and the need for more already eating away at his gut, he was beginning to have second thoughts about confronting Dingo. Maybe his best bet would be to just buy some more whiskey and ride off, exactly as he had planned in the first place.

A mongrel dog came running from behind one of the buildings, yapping and snapping at the heels of Percy's horse. The horse grew skittish and began kicking at the dog, prancing away from it, and Percy had to fight to keep the animal under control.

Regaining control, Percy stopped in front of the saloon and tied his horse off at the rail. From inside he heard a woman's short, sharp exclamation, followed by loud boisterous laughter from several men.

"That wasn't funny!" a woman's voice said. Her protest was met with by more laughter.

Percy went into the saloon and stepped up to the bar. First things first, and the most important thing on his mind right now was getting a drink.

"Mister, if you've come lookin' for a handout, you've come to the wrong place," the bartender said from the other end of the bar. "We don't give away drinks here."

Percy put his coin on the bar with a snapping sound. "Will this get me a drink?" he asked.

"Well. A drunk with money," the bartender said. "Yeah, hell, that'll get you a drink. A drunk's money is as good as anyone else's money, far as I'm concerned."

"That's pretty big of you," Percy said.

Percy looked at his reflection in the mirror behind the bar. He couldn't remember the last time his clothes had been cleaned . . . or even the last time he had taken them off. He knew that he reeked of every odor imaginable, but he had long since grown so used to the smell that he was no longer even aware of it. There were so many layers of dirt and filth that he couldn't even see his skin.

The bartender poured a shot of whiskey for Percy, then started to walk away.

"Leave the bottle," Percy said.

The bartender held the bottle back. "You got enough for a whole bottle?" he asked.

Percy put two dollars on the bar.

"This is good whiskey," the bartender said. "It's going to cost you more than two dollars."

"It's rotgut, colored with rusty nails and flavored with iodine," Percy said. "You figured, being a drunk, I wouldn't know the difference. I do know the difference, but I've reached the point to where it doesn't matter. Take my two dollars and leave the bottle, or leave the two dollars and take the bottle. It's up to you."

"Pretty highfalutin talk, comin' from a drunk."

"I wasn't always a drunk."

The bartender thought about it for a moment, then, with a shrug, picked up the two dollars and left the bottle sitting on the bar.

Percy poured himself two more drinks before the shakes stopped and the ache in his gut eased. Only then did he allow himself to turn and look out over the room. He recognized many of them, had actually ridden the outlaw trail with some. Seeing them here didn't surprise him.

"Jesus, Keith, look at you," a voice said. "What the hell happened to you? You're a damn drunk."

The speaker was Angus Dingo, and Percy smiled. He had thought he might find Dingo here, and he was right.

"You know what happened to me," Percy said. "It was the kid."

"What kid?"

"The little girl that was killed when we did that job in Rock Springs. If we hadn't been there that day, it wouldn't have happened," Percy said.

"And if a frog had wings, he wouldn't bump his ass ever' time he hopped," Dingo replied. "Those things happen."

"What about the Peabody kid?" Percy asked.

"The Peabody kid?" Dingo's face twisted in confusion.

"That didn't just happen. You killed him. Then you raped his sister while you made her parents watch."

"Where'd you hear that?"

"Are you saying you didn't do it?"

Dingo laughed. "No, I ain't sayin' I didn't do it, 'cause I did," he said. "I just didn't know their names, that's all."

"You raped the girl?"

Dingo laughed, then rubbed himself. "I had me a little party with the girl and her mama," Dingo said. They was fine, Percy. They was real fine."

Percy poured himself another drink, growing bolder and more disgusted with Dingo with each drink.

"Yeah," Percy said. "Well, we'll just have to see how fine it is when he catches up with you."

"He? Who he?" Dingo snorted what might have been a laugh. "You talkin' about the kid's ole man?"

Percy took another drink. He was as calm now as he had been in the days when he rode the outlaw trail.

"Nah, I ain't talkin' about him. I'm talkin' about John Slocum. I reckon you've heard of him."

The smile left Dingo's face. "Slocum?" He licked his lips nervously. "Why would Slocum be lookin' for me? He ain't gone into bounty hunting, has he?"

"Near as I can figure out," Dingus said, tossing down still another drink, "he's lookin' for you so he can kill your sorry ass."

"How does he even know about me?"

" 'Cause I gave him your name. I just wish now I had told him where to find you."

The expression on Dingo's face changed once again, going from fear, to anger, to rage.

"You? You gave him my name?"

Suddenly Percy realized that he had carried his taunting too far. The whiskey had been talking for him and he wished he could call it back. The hair stood up on the back of his neck, his insides turned to mush, and he soiled his pants. A twitch in his cheek began jerking, convulsively.

"You son of a bitch!" Dingo roared. "Draw!"

Percy had long ago hocked his pistol for whiskey, and he wasn't armed. He held his hands out in a gesture to show that he was unarmed, and a plea for mercy.

"No, no! I ain't got a gun!"

"No gun?"

"No!"

"You cowardly son of a bitch! You come in here to taunt me like this, and you ain't even carryin' a gun?" With a yell of anger, Dingo shot Percy.

The bullet hit Percy in the shoulder, slamming him back against the bar. He stood there for a moment, then, feeling himself about to fall, reached for the nearest thing he could grab to keep him up. His fingers wrapped around the neck of the now nearly empty whiskey bottle. As he fell, he pulled the bottle over so that the whiskey began pouring over him as he lay on the barroom floor. The bartender, not wanting to waste the whiskey, reached over quickly and set the bottle back up.

"What'd you shoot him for?" one of the saloon patrons asked. "He told you he wasn't carrying a gun."

"Hell, I didn't kill him. I just winged the son of a bitch."

"It don't matter whether you killed him or not. You know'd he wasn't wearin' no gun and you shot him anyway."

"You heard what he done, didn't you? He gave my name to John Slocum." Dingo looked over at Percy, who was now sitting up, but leaning against the bar, groaning.

"Dingo, we ain't got many rules in Brimstone," one of the others said. "But what ones we got, all of us follow."

"Yeah," still another said. "And one of them rules is, we don't go shootin' each other down in here, 'lessen both sides has a gun."

"I think maybe you'd better move on," the first man said.

"You heard what he done. He gave my name to John Slocum."

"All the more reason you need to move on. I've seen Slocum in action. He ain't someone you want to have ag'in' you, and I'd just as soon not have someone like him come to town."

"Listen, if we all stuck together, there ain't nothin' Slocum could do to me. I mean, if we all stuck together, we could kill him easy."

"He ain't our problem, Dingo. He's your problem. Now

my advice to you is to get. And don't come back 'till you ain't got no problem no more."

"What if I don't want to go?"

"Then we'll kill you where you stand," another man said, and turning, Dingo saw that nearly everyone in the saloon was pointing their guns at him. Two of them were holding double-barrel shotguns.

"Have one on the house, for the road," the bartender said. He was still holding the bottle Percy had bought, having preserved at least a fourth of it, before it all drained out. He poured Dingo a shot from what was left.

"Hey! That's my whiskey!" Percy said, reaching for the bottle and grunting with pain from the exertion. Retrieving it, he began drinking straight from the bottle.

"Look at him," Dingo said, derisively. "He's a damn drunk. You're going to let a drunk stay here, but you're running me out? I thought we was all friends here."

"People like us got no friends, Dingo. Just enemies. Hell, them two you're runnin' with ain't even your friends. Have you seen either of them take a hand in this?"

Dingo looked toward a table in the corner where Kelly and Pablo were staring pointedly into their drinks, trying to stay invisible.

"When you go, take them with you."

Dingo glared at the saloon patrons, and at the bartender. Then he took the glass the bartender offered him and tossed it down.

"I guess I'll be goin', then," Dingo growled.

"I guess you will."

"Come on," he called to Kelly and Pablo. "Let's find us a place where we're welcome."

"Hey, Dingo!" one of the men shouted as the three men started toward the door.

"Yeah?" Dingo turned back toward him.

"I hear tell there's a warm place for you down in hell."

Everyone in the saloon laughed as Dingo, his cheeks flaming in anger and embarrassment, pushed through the batwing doors and out into the sunshine.

The first pink fingers of dawn laced the eastern sky, the light was soft, and the air was cool. Slocum liked it best early in the morning. The last morning star made a bright pinpoint of light over the Salt River Range, purple mountains lying in a ragged line to the west.

The coals from the campfire of the night before were still glowing and Slocum threw a few chunks of mesquite wood onto it, then stirred the fire into crackling flames that danced merrily against the bottom of the suspended coffeepot. A lizard scurried beneath a nearby mesquite tree, which was itself dying under the burden of marasitic mistletoe.

Slocum poured himself a cup of coffee and sat down to enjoy it. It was black and steaming, and he had to blow on it before he could suck it through his lips.

The three women were still asleep in their bedrolls. To Slocum's surprise, Marie had not come to him last night. He didn't want to admit to himself, and especially not to her, that he had lain awake for some time, waiting for her. He was sure that she would come to him, because it was her turn. He didn't know whether she fell asleep and forgot about it, or if for some reason she just didn't want to do it.

It had been a while since Slocum was in this part of the country, but he knew that they were fairly close to a town called Brimstone. And though he had no way to be sure, Slocum would bet money that Dingo and those with him had gone to Brimstone. He knew they had money, and they would want someplace to spend it. Brimstone was that place.

Whereas most towns wanted to keep out the outlaw element, Brimstone welcomed such people. The merchants of the town had made a conscious decision to cater to the outcasts, enjoying an exclusive market as the result. And, because they charged inflated prices, they were growing rich from their unholy alliance with the worst elements of Western society.

Hearing a rustling sound behind him, Slocum turned to see that the three women were just beginning to stir.

"Well, I was wondering if you were going to sleep all day," he teased.

"All day? What do you mean, all day? It's still the middle of the night, for crying out loud!" Danielle squealed in protest. "Look, the sun isn't even up yet."

"It will be soon."

"Uhmm, I smell coffee," Delilah said.

"Help yourself. There are biscuits, too," Slocum said.

"What? You made biscuits? John, you would make someone a wonderful husband!" Danielle teased.

"Perhaps," Slocum replied with a chuckle. "But I'm not applying for the job."

The women rolled up their blankets and tied them into a bundle, and lay them by their saddles. As they worked, Slocum looked directly at Marie. Feeling herself the target of his scrutiny, Marie looked away, unable or unwilling to meet his glance. Why hadn't she come to him last night?

"So," Danielle said, blowing on her coffee to cool it. "What do we do today? Do we continue moving west? Do we have a trail to follow?"

Slocum took a swallow of his own coffee, then studied Danielle and the other two over the rim of his cup.

"You three women are committed to helping me find Dingo, right?"

"Right!" Danielle answered.

"Yes!" the other two responded.

"How committed are you?"

"What do you mean?"

Slocum pointed west. Half a day's ride from here is a town called Brimstone."

"Brimstone? I've never heard of it," Danielle said.

"It's not on any maps."

Delilah laughed. "Are you saying Brimstone? As in fire-and-brimstone?"

Slocum nodded, without laughter. "Exactly. And it's well named, for if ever there was an earthly portal to hell, it would be Brimstone. Every robber, thief, murderer, and derelict in the country has been there at one time or another."

"And the law does nothing about it?" Marie asked.

"Or is it one of those towns without law?" Delilah asked. "I've heard of those towns."

"Oh, Brimstone has law, all right," Slocum said. "But its law is the code of the outlaw—the law of the gun. Pretty much anything goes as long as they don't do it to each other."

"Sounds interesting," Danielle said.

"Think so?" Slocum asked.

"Well, yes. I mean, such places are hedonistic, aren't they? And I'm nothing, if not a hedonist."

"I'm glad you think so," Slocum said. "Because I want you to go into town ahead of me." He looked at the other two women. "All three of you."

"All right," Danielle replied with a curious look on her face. "What do you want us to do there?"

"Why, I want you to do what you do best," Slocum

said. "I want you to go into business with Delilah and Marie."

"In other words, you want me to open a whorehouse in Brimstone," Danielle said.

"That's exactly what I want you to do. Men talk when they are relaxed and off-guard. And nothing gets a man more relaxed and off-guard than a visit with an accommodating woman."

Delilah laughed. "Well, if that's all it takes, we can be very accommodating, can't we, girls?"

The others answered in the affirmative, but Slocum noticed that, once more, Marie didn't look at him.

9

The night creatures called to each other as Slocum and the three women stood in a small grove of trees, looking toward Brimstone. A cloud passed over the moon and moved away, bathing in silver the little town that rose up like a ghost before them. A couple dozen buildings, half of which were lit up, fronted the street. The biggest and most brightly lit building in town was the saloon at the far end of the street.

They could hear sounds from the town, an out-of-tune and badly played piano, a dog's bark, and harsh laughter. Some woman raised her voice, launching into a private tirade about something, but sharing her anger with all who were within earshot.

The three women were changing from the denim trousers and cotton shirts they had been wearing into dresses that were more indicative of their profession.

Danielle and Delilah made no effort to shield themselves, changing in full view of Slocum. But Marie stepped behind a clump of bushes, emerging a few minutes later wearing a dress. When all three were dressed, Danielle came over to speak with Slocum.

"Give us twenty-four hours," she said. "By then I will have found a place to open my establishment."

"You think you can set up your business in that short a time?"

"John," she said, "in my profession one can set up a business in one minute. Give me twenty-four hours, and I'll have an entire house going."

"What about Marie?"

"What about her?"

"Does she understand what is expected of her in, uh, this line of work?"

"Of course she understands, silly. She was one of my most popular girls."

"I'm having a difficult time seeing that."

"You mean because she has not come to you? And she wouldn't let you watch her dress?"

"Something like that," Slocum said. "I mean, don't you think her behavior is a little strange, coming from someone who is a soiled dove?"

Danielle laughed out loud. "You don't understand, John. She is embarrassed around you."

"I make her embarrassed? How is that?"

"Delilah and I look at you as a delicious dalliance, and nothing more. But Marie sees you differently. She is younger and though she is in the profession, she still has a degree of girlish innocence about her. And, with that innocence, comes fantasies. Marie has fantasies about you, John Slocum."

Slocum laughed, nervously. "Why would she have fantasies when she can have the real thing?"

Danielle shook her head. "*Non, monsieur*. I'm afraid you do not understand the nature of a young girl's fantasies. They are not, like young men's, fantasies of sex.

Rather they are fantasies of things that can never be."

Slocum shook his head. "I don't understand."

"Consider why we are here. To avenge the death of Kathy Caulder."

"Yes, but what . . . ?"

Danielle held up a finger. "Remember, Kathy was once one of us. But she left the line to marry Ned Caulder, who, I believe, was once like you. A drifter, a man more at home with a gun on his hip than a work glove on his hand. And yet, he made the change. So did Kathy."

"Oh," Slocum said. He looked toward Marie. "You mean she . . ."

Danielle shook her head. "Don't worry yourself, John," she said. "Marie is a woman of intelligence. She knows the difference between fantasy and reality, between what is attainable and what is impossible."

"I hope so," Slocum said, looking over at Marie. It was almost as if the young woman knew they were talking about her. She kept her eyes averted, studiously avoiding their glance. "I wouldn't want her to get hurt from any misunderstanding."

Danielle put her hand on John's shoulder. "You are a good man, John Slocum. You are a man with a heart that is pure."

Slocum chuckled. "I'm pretty sure there are a lot of people who would argue with you about that observation."

"Danielle, we're ready," Delilah called.

Danielle walked back to her horse, then mounted, though with some difficulty, given the fact that she, like the other two, was wearing a dress.

"I'll come into town twenty-four hours from now," Slocum said. "Try and stay out of trouble until then."

•   •   •

The sight of three women riding into town was unusual enough to draw a great deal of interest. The fact that all three women were very pretty caused even more attention, and when the people of the town saw that the dresses were obvious advertisements for professional ladies of the evening, the excitement reached fever pitch. Men began pouring out of the buildings that fronted the main street, hurrying down the street on each side, looking on in curiosity and unabashed lust. By the time Danielle, Delilah, and Marie reached the front of the saloon, they were leading a parade of nearly one hundred men.

They stopped in front of the saloon, and Danielle leaned forward to pat her horse on the neck. That action, by design, showed the tops of her breasts, almost all the way to the nipples. Looking out at the crowd of men, she put on her prettiest smile.

"Tell me, *monsieurs*. If three women wanted to rent a house, who would we see?"

A pudgy, balding man stepped out of the crowd. "What do you intend to use the house for?" he asked.

"Oh, *monsieur*, for pleasure of course," Danielle replied with a broad smile.

Upon hearing that, the men cheered, whistled, and applauded.

"Unless, of course, this town has an ordinance against pleasure," Danielle said. Knowing the erotic effects of an exotic dialect, she came down heavy on the French accent.

"Miss, we ain't got an ordinance against anything," the pudgy man said, and everyone laughed.

"The house, *monsieur*?"

"I've got one. I'll get you moved in pronto."

"*Merci.*"

"Miss, once you three get moved in, how soon will it

be before you are open for business?" one of the men in the crowd called to her.

"Oh, we will be open for business right away," Danielle replied enthusiastically. "I see no reason to delay, do you?"

"No, none a'tall," he replied. He was already rubbing himself in anticipation.

When Slocum rode into town twenty-four hours later, in accordance with their plan, he had no trouble finding Danielle's Pleasure Parlor. There was no sign to point it out, but there were customers moving in and out in a steady line. It was obvious to Slocum that Danielle's House of Pleasure was the most sought-after place in town.

Dismounting, Slocum heard some of the men talking. "We should'a had us a place like this long before now," one of the men said. "I'd rather spend my money on women than on rotgut."

"What do you mean, Jenkins? Are you sayin' we ain't got no whores here for you to spend your money on? We got 'em here. We've had whores all along."

Jenkins spat, as if in disgust. "Yes, we've got 'em all right, and there ain't a whore within fifty miles but what's not so ugly she'd make a train take five miles of dirt road."

Slocum went to the head of the line.

"Hold on there, mister," one of the men called. "Just where do you think you're going?"

"Gentlemen, gentlemen," Danielle said, coming over to them and smiling sweetly. "This particular cowboy is a longtime friend and very valued customer. We always give him . . . special . . . treatment."

She emphasized the word *special* in a way that was pregnant with meaning, and nearly every man in the line got an extra twitch as he imagined just how special the treatment was. More than one wished there was some way he could watch.

"Come inside, cowboy," Danielle invited.

Not all went along with Danielle's request, and one started to protest but someone leaned over toward him and spoke quietly in his ear, nodding toward the front of the house as he did so. The first customer nodded, and made no further complaint. The whispered name "Slocum" was heard, passing from lip to lip.

"You have your choice of ladies," Danielle said.

Slocum looked over at Delilah and at Marie. He saw that Marie had a quiet, confident smile on her face. She knew he was going to choose her because he had already been with the other too. She gave a short, quick, intake of breath when she heard him speak.

"I'll have you," Slocum said, pointing to Danielle.

"Oh, how wonderful!" Danielle said, wriggling her shoulders in anticipation. "You won't be sorry. I promise you, cowboy, you won't be sorry."

Slocum caught a glance of Marie as he started toward the back of the little single-story house with Danielle. Marie was trying hard to hide the disappointment on her face.

10

When Slocum awoke the next morning, he was aware that something wasn't quite right. It took him a moment to figure out what it was, and he chuckled at the recognition.

In Slocum's experience, most of the western towns he visited had two personalities. One of the personalities manifested itself at night. Then the only sounds one heard were of revelry: laughter, music, raucous conversation, and shouts of anger. There was gunfire as well, but most of the time the guns were discharged in fun, though sometimes in deadly seriousness. Brimstone's night persona was no different from the other towns. It was the day persona that spelled the difference between Brimstone and all the other towns.

In the daytime most towns were alive with the sounds of commerce: a carpenter's saw, a blacksmith's hammer, the rolling of wagon wheels, the drumming of feet on board sidewalks, and the ringing of little doorbells as customers went in and out of stores.

That was not the case with Brimstone. As Slocum lay there with the morning sunlight streaming in through the window, he realized that he was hearing none of the sounds of daytime commerce. Instead, Brimstone was strangely quiet, as if the entire town was still in bed, sleeping off the previous night's revelry.

Swinging his feet over the edge of the bed, Slocum sat there for a moment, then ran a hand through his hair.

After Danielle had moved him to the front of the line last night, she reminded him that everyone thought they had come back here for a specific reason.

"In order to make it more realistic, don't you think we ought to do what everyone thinks we came back here to do?" Danielle asked, seductively.

Slocum agreed, not only that time, but again, later, when most of the customers were gone and Danielle returned for a second visit to his room. Slocum had been put up in an extra room, not one of those used for visiting customers. As a result, he was able to enjoy an entire night in a regular bed.

This morning, as Slocum made use of the pitcher and basin to clean up, he was aware of the smell of bacon and coffee. A few minutes later he stepped into the kitchen of the house to see Danielle, Delilah, and Marie already up. Danielle and Marie were sitting at the table, Delilah was standing by the stove.

"How do you want your eggs?" Delilah asked.

"We have eggs?"

"And bacon, and biscuits baking in the oven," Delilah replied.

"Great. I'll have them straight up."

"Marie, get him a cup of coffee," Delilah said.

Without a word, Marie got up from the table and, using the hem of her dress as a hot pad, picked up the coffeepot and poured a cup. Her eyes were averted as she handed him the cup.

"Thank you, Marie," Slocum said.

"You're welcome," Marie replied, her words almost a whisper.

Delilah brought Slocum's eggs.

"Umm, they look good," Slocum said.

"Why?" Marie asked. The word was almost a plaintive wail.

"Why what?" Slocum replied, puzzled by the strange question.

"Why do you find me so ugly, John Slocum? Other men don't think I'm ugly."

"What? No, of course I don't think you are ugly. What makes you think I do?"

"Because, last night, when you had the opportunity, you didn't . . . uh . . . you wouldn't . . . you chose Danielle instead of me!" she finished in a rush.

"What did you expect, Marie? You've made it plain by your actions that you don't want anything to do with me."

"No! No, I haven't!"

Slocum started to dispute her, then decided that, in this particular instance at least, silence was the better part of valor.

Danielle finally broke the uncomfortable silence with a bit of information she had picked up the night before.

"John, do you recall the man you told us about, the one you met back in Puxico?" Danielle asked. "Didn't you say his name was Percy Keith?"

"Yes. Why do you ask?"

"He's here," Danielle said.

"You must be mistaken. I gave him money so he could get away. I don't think he would risk coming here and confronting Dingo."

"He is here," Danielle said. "Dingo shot him. Several people have told me the story."

"Shot him? You mean he's dead?"

"No, he wasn't even badly hurt."

"How do you know?"

"Everyone was talking about it last night," Danielle said. "They say Dingo shot him, then the others ran Dingo out of town."

"Because he shot Percy?"

"Yes," Delilah said. "The way it was explained to me is, Percy wasn't carrying a gun, and about the only law they have here is that you can't shoot an unarmed man."

"That's one reason they ran him out," Marie said. "But there is another reason."

"What's that?" Slocum asked.

"You."

"Me?"

"It seems that Percy told Dingo you were after him. The town didn't want you coming around. They are afraid of you."

"Yes, that's what I heard, too," Delilah said. "And yet, they know you are here now, because many of them recognized you last night."

"Now that they know you are here, is there a chance someone might try to kill you?" Marie asked.

"There is always that chance."

"It must be frightening to be so well known," Marie said. "Someone could recognize you, and want to kill you, but you wouldn't know they were. They could kill you when you weren't expecting it."

"I stay alive by always expecting it," Slocum said.

"That's very frightening," Delilah said. "And you live with that all the time?"

"Yes. Listen, maybe I'd better have a few words with Percy Keith," Slocum said, purposely changing the subject. "Did anyone happen to mention where he is staying?"

"They say he's staying over at the livery," Danielle said. "He's earning his keep by mucking out the stables."

When Slocum went to Meeker's Livery Stable to find Percy, he was met by a man who identified himself as Meeker.

"You're John Slocum, aren't you?" Meeker asked.

"Yes."

"What are you doing in Brimstone? You aren't working for the law, are you? You doin' some bounty hunting?"

"No," Slocum replied. "Right now, I'm looking for Percy Keith."

Meeker laughed.

"What's so funny?"

"Here, everyone is scared to death because you are in town. They're all wondering who you are looking for, and it turns out you are looking for the drunk. What do you want him for?" Meeker asked.

"That's my business," Slocum said. "Do you know where he is?"

"Yeah, I know where he is. You'll find him passed out, facedown in a pile of horseshit out back," Meeker said. "And as far as I'm concerned, that's a good enough place for him. You know him?"

"I know him."

"You know him enough to pay me what he owes me?"

"He owes you money? How is that? I thought he was working for you."

"He's supposed to be. But the son of a bitch took an advance on his pay, got drunk, and ain't done a lick of work since. I was plannin' on lettin' him sleep in one of the stalls, too. Would'a been a nice place for him. But I ain't letting him stay if he don't earn it."

"You say he's out back?" Slocum asked, starting through the barn.

"Yes. You going to pay back the wages he took?"

"That's your problem," Slocum said.

As Meeker had stated, Percy was lying facedown in a pile of dung. Only the fact that his face was turned to one side kept him from suffocating.

"Damn, Percy," Slocum said under his breath. "You are one filthy son of a bitch."

Looking around, Slocum saw a large trough, filled with water. He reached down and, grabbing Percy by his belt, lifted him up. Half carrying and half dragging him, Slocum took Percy to the trough, then rolled him over into the water.

The shock of the water brought Percy to, and he began splashing and gasping for breath.

"Help! Help! I'm drowning!" he called.

"No, you're not drowning," Slocum said, pushing him back into the water. "Get some of that shit cleaned off of you."

"Hey!" Meeker shouted, coming out back. "My horses has to drink that water."

Slocum handed him two dollars. "When we're finished here, you can refill it," he said.

Percy kept trying to get out of the trough, but Slocum kept pushing him back into it until, finally, most of the surface dirt and manure was gone. Finally, he let him out. "Let's go," he said.

"Go where?"

"With me," Slocum answered without being specific.

Slocum led Percy, who was dripping wet, along the back of the row of buildings and houses until he got to the house at the end. This was the house occupied by Danielle and her girls.

"You ought not to be here," Percy said. "This is a dangerous place for you."

"Dangerous for you, too, from what I've heard. Now, take your clothes off and sit there," Slocum said, pointing to the steps at the back of the porch.

"What do you mean, take off my clothes? I can't do that. I'll be naked."

"Take 'em off," Slocum ordered.

Percy complied without further argument. Then, with his clothes removed, he sat on the back stoop with his head bowed, while Slocum pumped water into a big, cast-iron tub. Danielle came out onto the back porch.

"What is going on?" she asked. "Oh, *mon dieu!* I have never seen anyone so filthy!" she said when she saw Percy.

"You should have seen him before I cleaned him up."

"He is clean?"

"Cleaner than he was, but not as clean as he is going to be." When Slocum had the tub full of water, he picked up a bar of brown soap and dropped it into the tub. He followed the soap with a stiff-bristled brush.

"All right, Percy, get into the water and take a bath. And scrub yourself clean with that brush."

Almost as if in a haze, Percy crawled into the tub. He picked up the soap and the brush and began to wash himself, then he let out a howl and dropped the brush.

"I can't wash with this here brush! It'll take my skin right off!"

"Then you'll grow new skin and it'll be a might cleaner," Slocum said. "Do it, or I'll shoot you."

"You wouldn't really shoot me, would you?"

"I probably should anyway," Slocum said. "It may be too late to clean you up."

Percy started scrubbing himself, complaining loudly. Hearing the commotion, the other two women came to the door and, seeing Percy naked in the tub, both of them laughed.

"Marie, get me a bottle of whiskey," Slocum said.

Marie complied, and Slocum poured a drink for Percy, then handed it to him.

"Thanks, Slocum," Percy said.

"Scrub," Slocum replied.

Percy began scrubbing. Slocum gave him another drink, and another still, and soon Percy was not only giving himself a good scrubbing, he was singing.

"Enjoy it, Percy," Slocum said. "Because you aren't getting any more."

"I don't need any more," Percy said.

"Would you like something to eat?" Danielle asked.

"No, nothing to eat. But, I would like to find me a place to take a little nap."

"Do you have a place we can put him?" Slocum asked Danielle.

"I think there's enough room in the back of the pantry to put down a pallet," Danielle said.

"Do it. We'll let him sleep this off before we start questioning him.

"This way, Percy."

Percy stood up, his skin shining red from the scrubbing, but clean, perhaps for the first time in years. Then, almost as quickly as he stood, he dropped back into the water and looked at the three women who were standing around the tub, as if seeing them for the first time.

"What is it?" Slocum asked.

"Women," Percy said, pointing at the three.

"Yes, they are women."

"I'm naked."

"Yes, you're naked."

"Why, I can't go paradin' around naked in front of women."

"You've been naked in front of them for the last half hour," Slocum said.

"Ain't the same thing. I was down in the tub."

"There is no need for you to be embarrassed, *Monsieur* Keith. This is a whorehouse," Danielle said.

Percy looked at the three women. "You mean you three is whores?"

"Oui."

"We three?" Percy asked, not understanding Danielle's reply of *oui*.

Danielle laughed. "Yes," she said in English.

"Oh," Percy replied. Again he stood up and, this time, walked naked and unconcerned into the house. "Oh, well, I reckon that's all right, then. Bein' as you're all whore's an' all, I reckon you've seen naked men before."

"I reckon," Danielle said, mimicking him.

"What about his clothes?" Delilah asked, looking at the clothes with her face screwed up in disgust.

"Burn them," Slocum answered. "I'll get him some more."

"Burn them? I don't even want to touch them."

"I'll do it," Marie said. She picked up a mop and used it to get the clothes, dangling them from the end of the mop handle.

As Marie and Delilah took care of Percy's clothes, Danielle led the red-shining, naked man into the pantry where she put down a pallet of blankets and quilts.

"Let me look at your wound," Slocum said, leaning over to check the bullet hole. There was a scab over the entry and exit wound, but there was no sign of the wound festering.

"You're lucky it didn't fester on you," he said.

"They's a doc here that's pretty good at treatin' gunshot wounds," Percy said. "He made me a poultice to suck out the poison so's it wouldn't fester none."

"There," Danielle said, rising up from her task of making the bed. "I think you'll be comfortable there."

"I thank you, ma'am," Percy replied. He lay down on the makeshift bed and was asleep within minutes.

Then, with Percy snoring away, Slocum and Danielle went into the kitchen. Marie and Delilah were just coming in from outside.

"The clothes were too wet to burn, so we just left them out there so the sun can dry them," Delilah said.

"Good enough," Slocum replied.

"I baked some cookies," Marie said, shyly. "Would you like a cookie and some coffee?"

Slocum smiled at her. "Yes, that would be nice, thank you."

"Does that offer go for all of us?" Danielle asked. "Or just John?"

"It's for you as well," Marie said. Marie served cookies while Delilah poured the coffee.

"How can anyone ever allow himself to become such a drunk?" Danielle asked, nodding toward the pantry.

"Maybe he was always a drunk," Delilah said.

Slocum shook his head. "No, he hasn't always been like this."

"You know him?"

"I met him."

"When? Where?"

"A long time ago."

11

As they sat around the table drinking coffee, Slocum told them the story of Percy Keith.

The little town was hot, dry, and dusty. It had grown up in the middle of nowhere and now sat baking in the sun like a lizard. As the four riders approached the town, Percy Keith slipped his canteen off the pommel and took a drink. The water was tepid, but his tongue was dry and swollen. He wiped the back of his hand across his mouth, then re-corked the canteen and hung it back on his saddle.

"Before we take care of our business, we ought to refill our canteens," Percy told the others. "This water's beginnin' to taste like piss."

"We take the time to do that, someone's goin' to see us, then the next thing you know everyone's goin' to have a good description of us," the leader of the group replied.

"Hell, Billy," one of the others said. "You think they ain't goin to have a good description of us any-

way, the moment we rob that there bank of their'n?" He hawked up a spit. "Look there," he added. "I ain't got enough wet to spit."

"What we ought to do is get us a proper drink, over to the saloon," the fourth suggested.

"Good idea, Johnny, Terry," Billy replied. "Only, why don't we rob the bank first, then go over to the saloon for a nice drink?"

"Damn, Billy, that don't make no sense a'tall," Johnny said.

"Neither does what you people are sayin'. Look, if we do this like we talked about, we'll walk into that bank, have the money, then be out of here again afore anyone in this town knows what hit 'em. Then when we ride into the next town we can go in in style. We'll have enough money to swim in beer if we want to. Women, hotels, restaurants, some gamblin' money. Hell, we can do anything we want."

"You ever know'd anyone to get two whores at the same time?" Terry asked.

Johnny laughed. "Two whores? Hell, you ain't never had one yet, have you?"

"Why, sure I have, lots of times," Terry said. "Whenever I got the money, that is, which, most of the time, I don't have."

"Well, you fellas do what I tell you to do today and you'll have all the money you need . . . even enough for two whores at the same time if you think you can handle that," Billy said. "Now, let's get on with it. You boys check your pistols."

The men pulled their pistols and checked the cylinders to see that all the chambers were properly charged. Then they slipped their guns back into their holsters.

"Ready?" Billy asked.

"Ready," the others replied.

The three men rode into town, then pulled up in front of the small bank. Billy, Johnny, and Terry dismounted and handed their reins to Percy. Percy remained in the saddle and kept his eyes open on the street out front. Billy and the other two looked up and down the street once, then they pulled their kerchiefs up over the bottom half of their faces and, with their guns drawn, pushed open the door.

There were three customers in the bank when the robbers rushed in. Because of the masks on their faces and the guns in their hands, the customers and the bank teller knew, immediately, what was going on.

"You fellas! Get your hands up and stand over against the wall!" Billy shouted to the customers.

The three customers complied with the orders.

Billy hopped over the railing to go behind the teller cage, then held his sack out toward the teller. "Put all your money into this sack," he growled.

Trembling, the teller emptied his cash drawer.

"They ain't much there," Billy growled.

"The rest is in the safe," the teller said.

"Open it."

"I beg your pardon?"

"Open the safe."

"I can't do that. I don't know the combination."

"What do you mean you don't know the combination? You work here, don't you?"

"Yes, but Mr. Edwards owns the bank. And he's the only one who knows the combination."

"All right, get him."

"He's out of town for the day," the teller replied.

"He won't be back until late this evening."

Suddenly the front door opened and Percy stuck his head in.

"Let's go, quick!" Percy shouted. "Somebody seen these fellas with their hands up and went runnin' down the street shoutin' about it. The whole town's been warned."

"Open the safe!" Billy shouted, pointing his pistol toward the teller and cocking it.

The teller began to shake, uncontrollably. "Mister," he said, "don't you think I would if I could? I don't want to die for someone else's money. I can't open that safe."

With a shout of frustrated rage, Billy brought his pistol down on the teller's head. With a groan, the teller dropped to the floor. Then, with the sack of money firmly clutched in his hand, Billy vaulted back over the teller's counter.

"Let's go!" he shouted.

As they reached the front door of the bank, someone from across the street fired at them with a heavy-gauge shotgun. The charge of double-aught buckshot missed the robbers, but it did hit the front window, bringing the glass down with a loud crash.

Billy shot back and though he missed the man with the shotgun, he at least drove him back inside. The bank robbers leaped into their saddles then started, at a gallop, down the street.

There had been several citizens out in the street and on the sidewalks when the shooting erupted, and now they stood there watching in openmouthed shock as the men who had just robbed their bank were getting away.

Slocum had been in the barbershop when the robbery took place, and now he came out onto the porch in front of the barbershop, still wearing the apron the barber had tied around him. Surmising quickly what had happened, he pulled his pistol. From here, it would be easy to shoot down all four of them.

Suddenly a small boy, either excited or frightened by all the activity, darted out into the street. His path took him right in front of the galloping bank robbers.

"Michael!" his mother screamed, starting after him.

"Stay back, Edna!" someone shouted, grabbing the woman. "You'll be trampled to death!"

"Michael!" Edna screamed again, fighting to go after her son.

Michael suddenly realized the danger he was in, but he was too frightened to move. He stood in the middle of the street, mesmerized by the sight of four horses pounding toward him.

Slocum had a notion to go after the boy, but at this stage he knew it would be suicide to try. The bank robbers were going to run the child down and there was nothing he could do to prevent it.

Suddenly one of the robbers cut in front of the other three, then leaned down from the saddle of a galloping horse, and scooped the boy up.

"Percy! Have you gone crazy? What the hell are you doing?" one of the others shouted.

As the others galloped off, Percy rode across the street, straight for the barbershop. There, he stopped his horse and set the boy down, right in front of Slocum.

"Get up on the sidewalk," he said. "Stay out of the street."

"Get off your horse," Slocum said, cocking his pistol and pointing it at Percy.

With a sigh of surrender, Percy dismounted, then he put up his hands.

Within seconds the townspeople converged on Percy. Capturing him, they dragged him down to the jail. It wasn't until an hour later, while Slocum was having a beer in the saloon, that he learned the town intended to lynch Percy.

"Why would you do that?" he asked. *"Nobody was killed, and if he hadn't stopped to help the kid, he would have gotten away with the others."*

"Yeah, but he didn't get away," someone said.

"And the kid wasn't killed."

"You got no say in this, mister. You're a stranger in town. It was our bank that was robbed, not yours. We want every outlaw in the country to know that you don't come to our town to rob a bank."

"I do have a say in this," Slocum said. *"I'm the one that captured him. I didn't capture him to see him lynched."*

"You ain't goin' to see it," someone said from behind him, and before Slocum could react, he saw lights and felt an excruciating pain as someone hit him over the head.

When Slocum came to a few minutes later, the saloon was nearly empty. Only the bartender was still inside.

"What's going on?" Slocum asked, so dizzy from the blow that for a moment he was confused as to where he was and what had happened.

"You weren't killed, huh?" the bartender said. Without being asked, the bartender poured a glass

of whiskey and handed it to Slocum. "Here, you probably need this."

"Thanks," Slocum said. He looked around the empty saloon. "Where is everyone?"

"They're down to the feed store, throwin' a rope over the hayloft stanchion. That's about the only place they can hang the feller you caught."

"Damn!" Slocum said. "They're lynching him!"

"They are, if they ain't already done it," the bartender said.

Slocum moved quickly toward the front door.

"May as well save your energy, mister," the bartender called to him. "Even if they ain't done it yet, you ain't goin' to get there in time."

Mounting his horse, Slocum pulled his rifle from its saddle scabbard, then looked down toward the feed store. He saw Percy Keith sitting in a saddle on his horse, just under the stanchion. There were several men standing around, watching, and jeering. Just above the stanchion, standing in the window that opened onto the hayloft, was a man, holding a rope. He leaned out to drop the rope over the arm, but as he did so, Slocum fired. His bullet hit the floor beside the man, kicking up bits of straw and dust before whining through the loft and out the other side.

"What the hell?" the man with the rope shouted.

"Drop the rope!" Slocum yelled.

"What? I'll do no such—"

Slocum fired again. This time the bullet took off the man's hat.

"Son of a bitch!" the man shouted in fear. Dropping the rope, he ran back into the loft, out of sight.

"You, the one standing beside Keith," Slocum shouted. "Cut his hands free." Slocum punctuated his order by pointing the rifle at the man standing nearest Percy Keith's horse. Without protest or comment, the man meekly complied with Slocum's order.

"Keith, ride toward me," Slocum said.

Free now, Percy rubbed his wrists a few times, then rode his horse toward Slocum.

"Thanks," he said, when he drew even with Slocum.

"Don't thank me," Slocum growled. "If I had my way, you'd be in prison for about twenty years. But it looks like these folks aren't going to let that happen. And since I'm the one captured you, I don't intend to let them lynch you. Now go. Get out of here."

"If there's ever anything I can do for you. . . ."

"Nothing you can ever do for me, bank robber," Slocum said with a growl. "Now get out of here before I change my mind."

With a nod, Percy slapped his legs against the side of his horse and galloped out of town. Slocum backed his own horse down the street for several more yards, all the while keeping his rifle pointed toward the lynch mob. Then, when he was sure he had a long enough start, he turned and galloped away from town as well, going the opposite way from Percy Keith.

"Oh, my! Did they come after you?" Danielle asked, when Slocum finished his story.

"No," Slocum answered. "I figured it would take them a minute or two to decide who they wanted most, the man they nearly lynched, or the man who helped their would-be victim get away. By the time they figured out who they wanted, it was too late for them to come after either one of us."

"Did you ever see Percy Keith again?"

"No. Not until I saw him in Puxico the other day."

"That's an interesting story, but it still doesn't explain what happened to him."

"Well, he caught up with the others, went back to riding the outlaw trail again," Slocum said. "Then, according to the story I heard, he and some others pulled a bank robbery back in Rock Springs, Wyoming. There was a lot of shooting, and one of the bullets went through the window of a dressmaker's shop. There was a little girl in there, with her mother. The little girl was killed."

"That's . . . that's almost like what happened in the story you told, isn't it?" Marie said.

"Yes. Only in Rock Springs, there was no happy ending."

"But, I don't understand. You said there was a lot of shooting. Was it Percy's bullet that killed the little girl?"

"Nobody knows," Slocum said. "And that's what started eating away at him. He gave up the outlaw trail then, but he was already in it too deep to come back. There were wanted posters out for him, all across the west. Without outlawing, and with no way to make an honest living, Percy sort of came down in between. He started drinking then, and he's been drunk ever since."

12

It was late afternoon before Percy woke up. When he did, it was to the smell of cooking pork chops.

"What is that smell?" Percy asked, coming out of the pantry. "It's killing me."

"Nonsense," Delilah replied. "There's nothin' smells better than pork chops, frying in the pan." She pointed to a pair of denim trousers and a blue cotton shirt. "By the way, you might want to put those on," she added.

"What the hell!" Percy shouted in alarm, trying to cover himself. "What am I doing here naked?"

Delilah laughed. "Being naked didn't seem to bother you when you came here."

Turning his back to preserve what modesty he could, Percy pulled on the trousers, then the shirt.

"That's another thing," he said. "Where is here? And how did I get here?"

"I brought you here," Slocum said, coming into the kitchen then.

"Slocum!"

"You goin' to make some gravy with that?" Slocum asked Delilah.

"Of course I am. You can't have pork chops without gravy."

"I'm going to be sick," Percy said.

"Not here, you aren't," Marie said. "If you feel sick, you just march yourself out to the back porch."

Percy went outside, then began throwing up over the back of the porch.

"Oh, that poor man," Marie said.

"Poor man?" Danielle asked. "He brought it all on himself."

"I suppose he did," Marie replied. "Still, you can't help but feel sorry for him."

Slocum and the women were halfway through their meal of pork chops, fried potatoes, biscuits, and gravy when Percy came back into the kitchen.

"There's a plate here, for you," Marie said, pointing to an empty plate.

"No," Percy said. He went back into the pantry and lay down on the pallet Danielle had made for him.

For the next several minutes, no one paid any attention to Percy. Then, when the meal was all eaten and Marie and Delilah began cleaning off the table, Slocum called into the pantry.

"Percy, whenever you are up to it, I'd like to ask you a few questions," Slocum said.

Percy gave no indication that he heard Slocum.

"Percy, you hear me?"

Still no response.

Danielle walked into the pantry and looked down at him.

"John?" she said.

"What is it?"

Danielle leaned over Percy and put her hand down to feel his neck.

"John," she said. "Come in here and look at him. I think he's dying."

Slocum and the others went into the pantry to look down at Percy. He was lying in the fetal position, and his trembling had become convulsive. His skin was leaden, and when John lifted one of his eyelids, he could see that Percy's eyes were rolled way back in his head.

"Damn," Slocum said. "He's dying of the deliriums."

"I know an old Cajun cure that might work," Danielle suggested.

"Try it," Slocum said. "We can't afford to let him die until we get some information from him."

"That's the trouble with this method," Danielle said.

"What's the trouble? What do you mean?"

"It'll either cure him, or kill him. And you never know which way it's going to go."

Slocum rubbed his chin and looked at Percy. Finally he sighed. "Do it. He's going to die anyway if we don't do something. We might as well take the chance."

"All right. I'm going to need the gunpowder from about eight bullets."

"I can take care of that," Slocum said. He slid eight .44-caliber shells from the loops of his pistol belt, then he handed them to Marie. "Take the powder out," he said. Then, to Danielle he asked, "What else do you need?"

"Some cayenne pepper, a bit of quinine and coffee, and a little grease. The pork gravy will take care of that."

"I'll have to go down to the store to pick up the cayenne and quinine," Delilah said.

"Hurry back," Danielle said. "There's no telling how much longer *Monsieur* Keith can stay alive."

Slocum waited anxiously for Delilah to return. She was back inside of ten minutes, and shortly thereafter, Danielle announced that she had everything ready.

"We'll have to give him one more drink to bring him out of the shakes and trembles," Danielle said. "When he comes out of that, we've got to make him drink the whole cup."

Marie looked at the concoction Danielle had put together, and wrinkled her nose.

"I'm glad it's him and not me," she said.

"I don't know if a sober person could even drink it," Danielle said.

"Here's a bottle of whiskey," Delilah offered. "How much should we give him?"

"Better give him a whole glass," Slocum suggested. "It'll take that much to bring him around."

Delilah poured an entire glass, then handed it to Slocum. Slocum held the glass under Percy's nose, and just as he thought it would, the smell caused Percy to start coming around.

"Here," Slocum said. "Drink this."

Percy opened his mouth and Slocum poured the whiskey in him. His throat worked automatically, gulping the liquor down. As they had hoped, Percy began coming around after the whiskey. The trembling stopped and he was even able to sit up.

"Thanks," Percy said in a hoarse voice.

"Here, I've got another drink for you," Slocum said, holding the concoction out to him.

Almost as a reflex action, Percy reached for the cup. He drank about half of it before he realized what he was drinking. When he started to gag in protest, Slocum forced his head back while Danielle poured the rest of it down his throat. After that, Percy began shaking and trembling, then he lay on his side with his knees drawn up, holding his stomach and moaning.

"It'll take a while," Danielle said.

It took all night. Slocum stayed back in the pantry with Percy during the night, even as the girls entertained their customers. Then, when everyone awoke the next morning they were gratified to see that Percy was still alive.

He was not only alive, he was in much better shape than he had been the day before. Though his face was still pinched and drawn, his eyes were open and clear. Percy sat on a chair in the kitchen while Marie cooked flapjacks for their breakfast.

"What about you, *Monsieur* Keith?" Marie asked. "Shall I make any of these for you?"

"I could eat a few," Percy replied.

When he answered in the affirmative, everyone knew that he was out of danger.

Percy ate more than just a few flapjacks. He had eight, gulping them down as fast as they appeared on his plate.

"It's going to take three of us cooking, just to keep you fed," Marie said as she brought more pancakes to him. "You act as if you hadn't eaten in days."

"Yes, ma'am, I reckon I do," Percy said.

"How long has it been since you've had a good meal?" Delilah asked.

Percy paused with the fork halfway between the plate and his mouth. He thought for a moment, then he shook his head. "I don't rightly know, ma'am," he said. "Can't remember eating anything."

"Well, you had to have eaten something. You can't stay alive on just whiskey."

"I reckon that's so," Percy agreed. "I just don't recall

eatin' anything." He smiled up at Marie. "And I know I ain't ever et anything this good. You make good flapjacks, ma'am."

"Percy, do you feel up to answering a few questions?" Slocum asked.

Licking the syrup off the end of his fingers, Percy nodded. "Yeah," he said. "I'll answer what I can."

"Do you have any idea where Dingo and the others might have gone?"

"Dingo has a cabin some west of here," Percy said.

"Dingo has a cabin?" Delilah said. "That's funny. Somehow I don't picture Dingo as being a settler."

"He's hardly what you'd call a settler, ma'am. The cabin used to belong to a fella by the name of Martin. Dingo allowed as how Martin and his wife sold the cabin to him, then went out to California, but I think he may have killed them."

"What makes you think that?" Slocum asked.

"Dingo ain't never struck me as a man who would buy anything, if he could figure out another way to get it."

"Where is this place?"

"It's near a little town called Salcedo."

"Salcedo? Is that where he gets his supplies?"

"Sometimes," Percy said. "But most of the time he'll just take what he needs, from farmers if has to. Who he really likes though, is immigrants."

"Who?"

"You know, travelers. Say a man an' his family is passin' through on a wagon. That's just like wavin' a red flag at a bull as far as Dingo is concerned. Wagons, and ranches or farms that's just got a few people livin' there, is all fair game for him."

"Percy, I know you aren't pure as the driven snow,"

Slocum said. "But how in the world did you ever hook up with someone like Dingo?"

"I first run into Dingo durin' the war," Percy said. "He called hisself a Confederate, but truth is he wasn't for no one but his ownself. There was lots of killin' done durin' the war, but Dingo done it even when it didn't need to be done. He likes it. And he likes rapin' women. Even if a woman is willin', like say a whore . . ." Percy suddenly stopped in mid-sentence and looked at the three women. "No offense meant, ladies."

"None taken," Danielle assured him.

"Go on," Slocum said.

"Well, like I was sayin', even if it is a whore who is willin', Dingo would rather rape her anyway."

"What about the two men who are with him?"

"The half-breed's real name is Pablo Goxando, but most just call him the breed. He has an Indian ma and a Mexican pa. His pa used to get drunk and beat up his ma, an' when the breed was twelve years old, why, he waited until his pa was passed out drunk, then he slit his throat. All three of 'em are good shots with a rifle or a pistol, including the breed, but what the breed really likes is the knife. He likes to cut people up."

"And the Irishman?"

"Kelly O'Riley. He deserted from the Yankee army. He was a sergeant, and him and two privates was supposed to take a payroll to his company commander. There was near two thousand dollars in the payroll, so O'Riley decided to keep the money for his ownself. He killed the two privates and skedaddled.

"I used to think it was strange that O'Riley and Dingo was friends. I mean, Dingo called hisself a Confederate, and O'Riley was a Yankee. But then I got to thinkin' on it some, an' I figured that it weren't no more'n just happenstance what they was. I mean, neither one of them ever really cared who won the war. They was just out for themselves."

"Whereas, you were a true patriot, right, Percy?" Slocum asked sarcastically.

"I was when I first got into the war," Percy insisted.

Slocum rubbed his chin, then looked at the others. "I've chased a lot of men," he said. "But it's been a while since I was after anyone I wanted as much as I want these men."

"What do we do now?" Danielle asked.

"I guess the next thing is to go to the cabin Percy told us about. You think you can find the cabin?" he asked the other man.

"Yeah, I think I can find it. But I'd rather just tell you where it is, than show you. There's only one way into it, and anyone who approaches can be seen from the cabin, long before they get there. The cabin is set back in a canyon so that only the front is exposed. It would take an army to get them out of there. That's why Dingo wanted it."

"I didn't figure it would be easy," Slocum said.

"I have an idea," Danielle said.

"What is it?"

"Where did you say he went for supplies? Sal something?"

"Salcedo. It's a town not too far from the cabin," Percy replied.

"If we go to the cabin, he will see us, and be prepared for us," Danielle said. "But, if we wait for him in Salcedo, he won't be expecting us."

"Us?" Percy said. "What do you mean, *us*? You mean, you women are going?"

"Yes, we are going," Delilah said.

"Why?" Percy asked.

"He raped and murdered a friend of ours," Marie explained.

"That's no reason for you to get yourselves killed," Percy said. He looked at Slocum. "You plan to let these women go with you?"

"Yes."

"You're crazy. You are all crazy," he said.

"Would you like some coffee, *Monsieur* Keith?" Marie asked sweetly.

"What? Uh, yeah. Yeah, thanks," he said. "And maybe, with a little whiskey in it?" he asked hopefully.

Slocum started to say no, but Danielle put her hand out to stop him.

"Why dilute good whiskey with coffee?" she asked. "Why don't you just drink it straight from the glass?" She poured a glass.

"Do you think that's . . ." Slocum started but again, Danielle put her hand out to stop him. Figuring she had something up her sleeve, Slocum grew quiet and watched.

"Thanks," Percy said, smiling as the glass was filled. He lifted it to his lips and took a drink.

The reaction hit almost immediately. Percy put the glass down and, grabbing his stomach, got up from the table and rushed out onto the back porch where he began to retch, loudly.

"What did you do to the whiskey?" Slocum asked.

"Nothing," Danielle replied, sweetly. "It's perfectly good whiskey. But that concoction we gave him last night has a long-term effect. For the next several days, every time he takes a drink of whiskey, he will react exactly as he did just now."

After a moment or two, Percy came back into the kitchen. "What did you put in that whiskey?" he asked, repeating Slocum's question.

"There is nothing wrong with the whiskey. See?" Smiling at him, Danielle took a large swallow from the glass.

"Let me have another swallow," Percy demanded. Taking another swallow, he reacted this time just as he did the first time and once more ran to the back porch. Finally, he came back in.

"You know what's happening to you, don't you, Percy?" Slocum asked.

Percy shook his head.

"The whiskey level has built up in your body until it has reached the point that it can no longer tolerate it. From now on, as far as you are concerned, whiskey is poison."

"Ohhh," Percy groaned, and he sat at the table with his head in his hands while Slocum and the women discussed how they would confront Dingo when he and the others came to Salcedo for supplies.

Percy listened for a few minutes, then he raised his head. "That's not how to do it," he finally said.

Slocum and the women looked at him.

"Do you have a better plan?" Slocum asked.

"I've got an idea, yeah," Percy replied.

"What is it?"

"I told you, even more than going into town to get supplies, he likes to take what he needs from immigrants. We could maybe get us a wagon, then pose as immigrants. Then, when he comes to raid the wagon, we'll be ready for him."

"*We* will be ready for him?" Slocum asked.

Percy ran his hand through his hair. "Yeah," he said. "I ain't been worth nothin' to nobody for a lot of years now. Maybe it's time I done something good. I'd like to go with you."

"You know what you are getting into?" Slocum asked.

"Yeah, I know."

"You could be killed."

"Yeah."

"What's worse is, we could all be killed. In fact, instead of helping us, having you along might make things worse."

"Please," Percy said. "Let me go with you."

Slocum stroked his chin for a moment, then put it to the three women. "What do you think?" he asked. "Shall we let him come with us?"

"I say yes," Marie said.

"I'm willing to give him a chance," Delilah said.

"I know what it's like to want to make up for something," Danielle added.

Slocum looked at Percy for a long moment, then he sighed. "All right, Percy, you can come with us," he said. "But understand this. If I get the slightest idea, if I even get nervous over whether or not you might turn on us, I'll kill you without blinking an eye. Do you understand that?"

"Yeah," Percy said. "I understand." He looked at Marie. "If you don't mind, miss, I'll have that coffee now."

"Of course," Marie answered.

13

Leaving the women's horses boarded at Meeker's Livery, Slocum and the others bought a wagon from him and were now two hours out of Brimstone on the Wilderness Road. Percy was driving the wagon with Marie sitting beside him. Percy was wearing overalls and a straw hat, while Marie wore a long, cotton dress and a bonnet. Slocum was also wearing overalls, and he appeared to be dozing as he rode alongside the wagon with a straw hat pulled low over his eyes.

In fact, Slocum wasn't dozing at all. His eyes were narrowed and alert, and he was ever mindful of the pistol he had stuck down in the deep pockets of his overalls. He was inviting attack by his appearance of lazy indifference. Indeed, he was hoping such an attack would come.

Slocum would have liked nothing better than to have Dingo, Goxando, and O'Riley before him. What Dingo had done to Ned and Kathy Caulder, and what all three of them had done to the Peabody family, made his blood boil. They had gotten away with it so far, but their time would come. Slocum was an avenging angel from hell, come to collect the devil's due.

It took them four days by wagon to cover the fifty miles from Brimstone to Salcedo. They could have made the trip in two days, but Slocum was in no hurry. He had hoped by his plodding pace to draw the outlaws into an attack.

But nothing happened.

Unlike Brimstone, Salcedo was a law-abiding town of enterprising merchants and commercial activity. The streets of the town were filled with good men and women going about their daily business. And, because it was a trade center for the surrounding agricultural area, a large number of wagons were pulled up to the stores, some loading, others unloading their goods.

Percy drove the wagon down the main street into the bright and sunny plaza, then stopped in front of the hardware store. Slocum stopped alongside, then looked around the town.

"What now?" Percy asked.

"Drive on through town and park on the other side," Slocum said. "I want you to stay with the wagon and out of sight. Danielle, you and the other ladies get out and wander around through town. See what news you can pick up."

"You mean I gotta stay in the wagon?" Percy complained.

"I don't want anyone recognizing you," Slocum replied.

Still dressed in his overalls, Slocum went into the hardware store.

"Yes, sir, what can I do for you?" the store clerk said.

"I need a little information, if you don't mind."

"Information is free," the clerk said. "And worth every penny of it," he added, with a laugh.

Knowing it was expected, Slocum laughed with him. "I've got my family in a wagon just out of town, here," he said.

"Yes, sir, I seen you folks comin' by a few minutes ago," the clerk replied.

"Well, the thing is, we're movin' through this part of the country and I've heard there is a gang of outlaws that sometimes preys on wagons."

The clerk's eyes narrowed slightly, then he looked around to see who was close enough to overhear him.

"Yes, sir, you got a right to be worried," he said. "They's four of the meanest critters you ever thought about out here. Well, no, only three now. Word is Flat-nose Nelson got hisself killed sometime back. But the other three is still here, and there ain't nothin' they like bettern' jumpin' a dirt farmer an' his family. An' it don't matter none whether the farmer's in a wagon or in his own house."

"I was afraid of that," Slocum said. "So, what road should I avoid, and what road should I take?"

"My advice would be to avoid Prairie Trail. Stay on the Wilderness Road as much as you can."

"Thanks," Slocum said. They had come by the Wilderness Road and nothing had happened, which verified the clerk's observation. Therefore when they left town, they would go by the very road the clerk had just told him to avoid.

On Prairie Trail ten miles west of Brimstone, Matt Dixon was driving a single wagon down a rutted road. His wife, Sally, sat on the seat beside him while their fifteen-year-old daughter, Verity, rode in the back, wedged in between boxes of clothing, a few items of furniture, household goods, a plow, and several more farming utensils.

"I wish you had waited until there were two or three more wagons wantin' to go in the same direction," Sally said. "I would feel a lot safer."

"We couldn't wait for another wagon," Matt said. "You know the situation. If the taxes aren't paid within five days, your uncle's land is going up for the sheriff's auction."

"So what if it does?" Sally replied.

Matt looked at his wife as if she had lost her mind. "Your uncle left that land to you and all we have to do to claim it is pay the back taxes. We got the money for the back taxes. But if it goes to auction, more'n likely we'll lose it. That's good land, Sally. It can set us up for life. Most people go a lifetime and don't get a chance like this."

"Why did we have to move, anyway?" Verity asked. "I won't know anyone there. It's going to be awful," she complained.

"Oh, a nice young girl like you? You'll meet new friends right away," Matt promised his daughter. "You'll see."

They didn't stop for lunch, but they did stop for supper. Sally opened a can of beans and cooked them with smoked ham. Verity made the corn bread.

"Uhmm, this is the best corn bread I've ever eaten," Matt said.

"You shouldn't say that, Daddy," Verity scolded, though her smile showed she was proud of the compliment. "Mama makes good corn bread, too. How do you think it makes her feel to hear you say that?"

Sally laughed softly. "It makes me feel very good to know that you have learned to cook as well as you have."

• • •

Ten miles behind the Dixon wagon, also on Prairie Trail, Slocum and his little party made camp for the night. Believing that his was the only wagon on the road, Slocum did everything he could think of to draw attention to them. Still dressed in denims and homespun, he had everyone parade around very visibly. Delilah could play the guitar and Marie the harmonica, so Slocum had them play as many rousing songs as they could, then, after nightfall, he left instructions for everyone who was on watch to keep the campfire burning brightly, all night long.

Danielle suggested, jokingly, that they make a big sign and leave it somewhere, reading WAGON WAITING TO BE ROBBED.

Even though it was forced party atmosphere, the women did seem to be enjoying themselves and they played the songs with a great deal of enthusiasm. Danielle even enticed Slocum to dance with her a couple of times.

Percy wasn't enjoying it at all. Although the concoction Danielle had whipped up made whiskey intolerable to him, he still had the need for a drink, and he was having a hard time with the shakes. He sat on the ground with his back against the wagon wheel, suffering through alternating spells of chills and fever.

"H-how l-long will I h-have to g-go through this?" he stuttered.

"You should be over it in a couple more days," Danielle promised.

"If I l-live that long," Percy replied morosely.

It was after midnight. A pocket of gas in a burning branch burst, sending a tumbling spray of sparks into the night sky. Catching a rising column of hot air, several of the tiny red embers climbed high enough to mingle with the stars. Overhead a meteor shot by, a flash of light zipping across the sky before fading into blackness.

Slocum lay in his bedroll watching the light display. He had taken the 10:00 to 12:00 watch, and though he was supposed to be sleeping now, he was in that stage he often reached at such times . . . quick dozes which, while providing him with some rest, nevertheless left him alert enough to know what was going on around him.

It was because he was in that state of awareness that he knew someone was sneaking through the night toward him. He knew, also, that the person crawling across the ground, meant no harm to him. It was Marie.

"John," Marie whispered. "John, are you awake?"

"I'm awake," Slocum replied, quietly.

Marie moved the last few feet until she was by his side.

"I think I owe you an apology."

"You don't owe me anything."

"I think I do. And I'd like to give it to you now," Marie said.

She crawled over him then, peppering his face with her kisses and reaching down to squeeze the cock that had awakened, quickly, to her ministrations.

The fire in Slocum's loins shot through him like lava from a volcano.

"Do you want to accept my apology?" Marie asked.

"Yes," Slocum said, his voice husky. "Yes, I'd like to accept your apology."

"I hoped you would," Marie said. In the orange light cast by the fire, Slocum could see Marie smiling. He could see, also, that she was stripping out of her dress. He slipped the straps down off his shoulders and slid out of the overalls he was still wearing and soon, both lay naked on the blankets, stripped like babies to bare flesh.

Slocum sucked a hard, rubbery nipple between his lips

while Marie's hand caressed his cock, sliding up and down its length. A warm clear fluid seeped from its tiny slit. Using the tip of her finger, she rubbed the wetness over the velvety ripples of the crown, squeezing it with an urgency that shot through him in fiery tingles.

Slocum looked down at the thatch between her legs. A light breeze caressed their naked bodies. Shadows from the campfire danced across their exposed flesh.

"Now," Marie said. "Put this in me, John."

Slocum rolled over on her, straddling her with his lean frame. She spread her legs and he sank his shaft into her, finding the pink through the muff of her pubic hair. She gasped as his swollen cock plunged deep into her.

Feeling the warm wetness of her, Slocum pushed himself in, pulled back, then plunged in again. He could feel shoots of pleasure coursing through him. Then he felt her shudder as her entire body jolted with a sudden, unexpected climax.

Marie's fingernails raked across his shoulders.

"Oh, John, I never knew it could be like this," she gasped. "I have done this, so many times before, with so many men, but, never has it been like this."

Again, orgasm burst over her and she bucked with the spasms, gasping in ecstasy.

"Don't stop," she said, "don't ever stop!" She was mindless now from the burning pleasure she was feeling, and she no longer made any effort to keep quiet.

Slocum drove in deep, and felt his seed boil. He exploded inside her, spurting and pumping his fluid until, at last, he grew limp.

They lay together for several moments afterward, gasping for air until, at last, their breathing returned to normal. Finally he rolled off her, and she pressed herself against him, putting her head on his shoulder. His arm wrapped around her, his hand easily, naturally, cupping her breast.

"Thank you," she said.

Slocum chuckled. "Actually, I'm the one who should be thanking you."

"No, I don't mean that."

"You don't?"

"Well, yes I do. It was good, John. It was better than anything I had ever experienced, and I thank you for that as well, but I knew it would be. No, what I'm thanking you for is for having patience with me. I know I have been acting like a spoiled brat, playing the game of a nervous virgin, keeping away from you. But through all of that, you have shown amazing patience, and it is for that, that I thank you."

"It was worth the wait," Slocum said. Gently, he squeezed her breast and ran his thumb over the nipple. He was surprised to feel another shudder of pleasure emanating from her. But he was even more surprised to realize that he was feeling his own rekindling.

Marie's hand was resting on Slocum's spent cock, and she felt it begin to stir anew.

"Oh, my," she said. "Oh, my, John." She began moving her hand up and down its shaft, and as she did so, it slowly began to unfold, lifting like an undefeated fighter rising from a blow that has knocked him down, but not out.

"Careful," Slocum said. "You might be starting something you can't finish."

"Oh, I can finish it all right, don't you worry about that," Marie said. Moving down his body, she took his cock into her mouth and began working it, applying suction, squeezing the sides, and flicking her tongue across its head. Slocum put his hands down to her head and held her to him, not forcefully, but gently.

It didn't take all that long.

14

They had been on the trail for the better part of two hours when Slocum shielded his eyes with his hand to look at the circling birds about two miles away. They were vultures, black messengers of death hanging on outstretched wings, waiting for their turn at some gruesome prize. Slocum knew it would have to be something larger than a dead rabbit or a coyote to attract this much attention. It could be an elk, or a horse, but from the way the birds were behaving, Slocum knew that it was more likely a man.

Slocum had seen vultures at work enough times to know their habits. He knew they had a certain way of circling over a human carcass. Vultures are basically cowards, and humans are the most terrifying of all creatures to them . . . even dead humans. As a result, the birds circle longer, make their descent more cautiously, hang back to let others go first. That was what these birds were doing.

"Slocum," Percy called.

"Yeah, I see them."

It took them another half hour to reach the objects of

the vultures' attention. From a distance they could see a
wagon, but no horses, and what appeared to be the contents of the wagon spread out across the ground. It wasn't
until they were closer yet that they saw the vultures' real
targets. Two bodies, not yet bloated and blackened by the
sun, lay on the ground alongside the wagon.

"Oh, *mon dieu!*" Danielle said, crossing herself.

"Dingo's work?" Slocum asked.

Percy rubbed his chin, then, nodded. "Yeah," he said.
"It looks like it."

Slocum, who was riding a horse alongside the wagon,
sighed, then dismounted. "We may as well get them buried," he said.

With the bodies buried, Slocum began looking around.
The contents of the wagon, a couple of plowshares, a sack
of seed corn, some carpentry tools, and other items of a
workingman were scattered about on the ground. It was
obvious that whoever attacked wasn't interested in any
item that had anything to do with work.

"John, look at this," Marie said, bringing a little ledger-
type book to him.

"What is it?"

"It looks like a diary," Marie said.

Slocum thumbed through the book until he reached the
last page. "What is today's date?"

"Don't ask me," Percy said. "I don't even know what
year it is."

"It's the twelfth of June," Danielle said.

"That means the last entry was made yesterday," Slocum said. He began reading aloud. " 'Mama and Papa
both say I am going to find new friends where we are
going. That may be true, but I know I will never have
another friend like Judy. She was my best friend in the

whole world. I hope she doesn't forget me.' She doesn't sign the entry."

"Look in the front of the book," Marie said. "If it's a diary, she probably put her name there."

Opening the book Slocum saw an entry that chilled his heart. *The story of our great adventure, by Verity Dixon, age fifteen.*

"Verity Dixon, age fifteen," Slocum said. "That's about the same age as the little Peabody girl."

"Maybe she's around here, somewhere," Danielle suggested.

"We can look for her," Slocum said. "But I think we'll just be wasting our time. I'm sure they've taken her with them."

"The bastards," Danielle said.

Slocum looked over toward Percy. "Tell me again about that cabin they have."

Percy shook his head. "If they're holed up in that cabin, it'll take an army to get them out."

"Yeah? Well, we are an army," Slocum said. "We just aren't a very large army."

"You call this an army?" Percy asked, taking them in with a wave of his hand. "Three whores and a drunk?"

"Are you drunk right now, Percy?" Danielle asked.

"What? No, I'm not drunk."

"And we aren't whoring," Danielle replied. "So it's like John said, we are an army. And an army does what its commander tells them to do. John, you are our commander. What do you want us to do?"

"First, we have to find where they've taken her," Slocum replied. "And my guess is they've taken her to their cabin."

●   ●   ●

If they had been mounted, they would have made the trip faster. As it was, it was nearly nightfall by the time the wagon reached the cabin.

"There it is," Percy said. "Just on the other side of the creek."

Percy pointed to a cabin. Alongside the cabin was a lean-to, and inside the lean-to, they could see three horses.

"They're here, all right," Slocum said.

"No! Please, don't!" The high-pitched cry of a young girl came from the house.

"They've got her! Those sonsofbitches!" Delilah said.

"They aren't going to get away," Slocum said resolutely. "Do you understand that? No matter what happens, they aren't going to get away."

"You don't know him like I do, Slocum," Percy said. "You don't know what kind of trick he'll pull. He's a slick one."

"He is a murdering raping, low-down son of a bitch," Slocum said. "And all the tricks in the world won't help him. He won't get away."

"What do you have in mind, John?" Danielle asked.

"Percy, is there a way out through the back of the cabin?"

"A window, but it would be a tight squeeze for anyone to get through it."

"Then the only way they can get out is through the front door," Slocum said. "And that means they aren't going to get out."

"Someone's coming out now!" Marie hissed.

The front door of the cabin opened and one of the men came outside. It was the breed, and he stood alongside the door to relieve himself.

"Shoot him," Delilah said. "Shoot the sonofabitch."

"No, not yet. If I shoot him, the others will kill the girl for sure."

"What are your going to do?"

"I'm going to give them a chance to surrender," Slocum said. He cupped his hands around his mouth and called to the cabin. "Dingo! O'Riley! Goxando!"

Even from this far away, they heard an exclamation of surprise from the cabin. It was obvious that Dingo and his men thought they were completely safe.

"Dingo!" Slocum called again.

"What do you want?" Dingo called back.

"I want you and your men to surrender."

"Are you Slocum? Are you the one that's been hound-in' me?"

"That's me," Slocum said.

"Well, Mr. Slocum," Dingo said. "What you might not know is, we've got us a girl in here. And iffen you don't back off, we're going to kill her."

Inside the cabin, Dingo looked around at the others. "Damn! Where'd that sonofabitch come from? How'd he find this place?"

"Who is this Slocum, anyway?" the breed asked.

"He's someone you don't want to mess with," O'Riley said.

"So, what do we do now?" the breed asked.

Dingo looked at the girl. "This here girl might be our only chance," he said. He moved over to the window and cupped his hands around his mouth.

"Slocum!"

"I hear you, Dingo."

"Slocum, you better get out of here," he shouted. "You better get out of here or we'll kill the girl."

"Then what?"

"What?" Dingo replied, confused by the answer.

"The girl is your only bargaining chip. If you kill her, then what will you do? You don't have anywhere to go, Dingo. Give it up. Give it up now."

"He's right, Dingo. We don't have anywhere to go," O'Riley said.

"Yeah? Well, let's just show him we can't be buffaloed. Drag the girl to the front door so's they can see you," Dingo said. O'Riley did as he was directed. "When I give you the word, cut her throat."

The door opened and O'Riley stood in it, holding the girl in front of him.

"I told you what I was going to do, didn't I, Slocum?" Dingo called to him. "This girl's blood is on your hands, not mine."

"Dingo, you don't have a chance in hell of getting out of here alive unless you . . ." Slocum stopped in mid-sentence when he saw what happened next. O'Riley pulled his knife across the girl's throat and a bright, red stream of blood poured from the slash. O'Rily dropped her, then stepped back inside. The girl fell to the ground and flopped around a couple of times, then lay still while a spreading pool of blood flowed from the wound in her neck.

"God in heaven!" Marie said.

Slocum had seen death in many guises and forms over the years, from the horror of warfare to the brutality of murder in the street. But this wanton slaughter of an innocent young girl made him gag, and he turned away, fighting against the urge to vomit. He sucked in air to quell the queasiness in his gut.

"What . . . what do we do now?" Danielle asked.

"We could wait them out," Delilah suggested.

"Is there water in that cabin?" Slocum asked Percy.

"Yes," Percy said. "There's a pump goes down to a well, comes up inside the house."

"And we know they have food, because they just robbed the Dixon wagon." He shook his head. "There's no way we can wait them out."

"We can't go in after them," Percy said. "They can pick us off while the heavy logs of the cabin walls will stop anything we can shoot at them."

"Logs," Slocum said. "Pine logs, aren't they?"

"Yes."

"Pine has lots of pitch," Slocum said. "And pitch burns, really, really well."

That night, moving like an Indian, and staying in the shadows so as not to expose himself, even to moon glow, Slocum crawled all the way around the cabin. He was now in position behind the little shack. Signs of the filth in which the men lived were scattered about everywhere. There were skins, feathers, and bones from game animals the men had killed and eaten. There was the sour smell of urine and the overwhelming stench of human excrement, evidence that, like animals, the men relieved themselves anywhere they felt the need. Taking shallow breaths and moving cautiously, Slocum finally reached the back of the house.

He had used the night to cover his movement, but, as he explained to the others, if they tried to leave now, they could use the cover of darkness to mask their escape. Therefore he decided to wait until morning before he put his plan into operation.

Slocum spent the night behind the house, several times fighting the urge to gag against the filth. Then, finally, dawn came and he was ready to put the plan into operation.

Using a small mirror he had borrowed from Marie, he caught the morning sun, then sent a flash of light toward the rocks where he knew the others were waiting. They returned his signal with one of their own and he knew they all were in place, and everything was ready.

Lighting a handful of small twigs he had gathered, he held a blaze underneath one of the logs. Rich in pitch, the log caught quickly, and within moments, a large flame was licking up the backside of the cabin. The horses in the lean-to started acting up then, frightened by the flames, and Slocum hurried around to let them go. Mounting one of them, he led the other two and galloped quickly back to the others before anyone in the house knew he had been there. He knew that it was less dangerous returning than it would be approaching the house, for all defense postures were directed toward the house being attacked, not toward someone running away. Therefore, Slocum was able to make it back before he was even seen.

By now the entire back wall of the cabin was invested in flames and some of the shakes on the roof were burning through.

"Fire!" someone inside the cabin shouted. "Fire!"

"When they come to the front door, start shooting," Slocum said. "Don't shoot them, I don't want them killed yet. Shoot around them, drive them back inside."

Slocum had scarcely gotten his word out when Dingo, O'Riley, and the breed started outside.

"Now!" Slocum shouted. Slocum and the others opened fire on the three outlaws. Bullets slammed into the walls around them, even into the door frame, and bits and pieces of splintered wood flew up from the impacts.

"Stop shooting! Stop shooting!" Dingo called. "Can't you fools see this cabin is on fire?"

"Surrender . . . or burn to death!" Slocum called out.

Once more Dingo appeared at the front door, and again bullets peppered the door frame and walls around him. Again, he was driven back inside.

"You sonofabitch!" Dingo shouted from inside.

"Throw your guns out," Slocum called. "Throw your guns out, then you can come out."

The breed made another try, also to be driven back by gunfire. By now the entire roof was ablaze.

"All right! All right, you win!" Dingo shouted. "We're givin' up! We're comin' outside, don't shoot!"

"Throw your guns out first," Slocum ordered.

There was but a moment's hesitation, then all three men tossed their guns through the front door. They followed their guns out, coughing and wheezing, holding their hands up in the air.

"Hold it!" Slocum called to them.

"We can't stay here," Dingo replied. "It's purt' near as hot here as it is inside!"

"Bring the girl's body with you," Slocum ordered.

Dingo said something and O'Riley and the breed bent down to pick up the girl. Then, even as the walls were collapsing behind them, they hurried out of the bubble of heat and toward the guns that were leveled on them.

15

Slocum made Dingo and the others dig a grave for Verity Dixon. Wrapping her in a blanket and poncho taken from one of the outlaws' horses, the girl's body was laid gently in the excavation, then it was closed, leaving a mound of earth to mark its location.

Danielle said a few words then, reminding God of the short and innocent life the young girl had lived on earth, and asking that she find her reward in heaven. Slocum, the other women, and even Percy, were paying respectful attention to the words, when Dingo suddenly grabbed Marie around the neck and started dragging her over to the edge of a hill.

"John!" Delilah shouted.

"Don't come any closer!" Dingo cautioned. "I'll break her neck if you do. And I reckon by now you know I don't bluff."

"John, don't mind me," Marie gasped. "Even if he kills me, don't let this son of a bitch get away! Not after all he has done!"

"He won't get away," Slocum said. "I promise you that.

Keep the other two covered," he ordered quietly.

If the other two outlaws held out any hope for their own escape, they were out of luck, because they suddenly found themselves looking down the barrels of the guns of Percy, Danielle, and Delilah.

"We ain't trying to go nowhere!" O'Riley said quickly, throwing up his hands.

"Oh, I'm sure you're not," Delilah said.

Dingo dragged Marie with him to the edge of the hill. Then Marie, with a quickness and strength that no one knew she had, pushed Dingo away from her. Dingo fell over the edge of the hill and rolled down to the bottom of the draw. Once he was on the ground he started running, certain now that his getaway would be successful.

"Look at ole' Dingo run," O'Riley said with a chuckle.

"He's acting like he's going somewhere," Slocum said with no show of emotion. Slowly and calmly, he walked back over to his horse.

"John, don't let him escape!" Danielle said.

"He won't escape," Slocum promised. He looked at the other two prisoners. "Remember, keep an eye on them."

"What are you going to do?" Danielle asked.

"I'm going to stop Dingo."

"How? He's got too good of a head start."

"I'll find a way," Slocum said. He pulled out his Winchester, then walked, almost casually, over to the edge of the hill. Dingo was still running hard, getting farther and farther away and growing more and more sure of himself. Slocum licked his finger, and held it into the breeze.

"Not much of a breeze," he said. "And what there is, is coming from the north. This ought to take care of it." Slocum made a slight adjustment to his rear sight.

Percy chuckled. "If you just let him run, the sonofabitch would run clear to Texas."

"I expect he would try, at that," Slocum said.

Slocum sat down on a flat rock, crossed his knees, then raised his rifle to his shoulder. On the floor of the gully, now some two hundred yards away, Dingo was still running.

"Are you going to kill him?" Danielle asked.

"Not if I can help it," Slocum said. "I have other plans for him."

"What plans?"

"You'll see. I'm going to try to wing him."

"You can't wing him from here," Percy said. "Not even you are that good."

"I'm going to give it one hell of a try," Slocum said.

Slocum took a deep breath, let half of it out, then drew a bead on the running figure. After a long moment, he squeezed the trigger. The rifle roared and rocked him back. A puff of smoke drifted out from the end of the barrel and when it rolled away, Slocum could see Dingo lying in the dirt.

"Good! You killed the bastard!" Delilah said.

"No, but that's what he wants us to think," Slocum said. "He's hoping we'll think he's dead and will just leave him there."

"Are you sure you didn't kill him?" Percy asked.

"I hit him in the lower leg, which is just where I aimed," Slocum replied.

Dingo continued to lie in the dirt, unmoving.

"Dingo," Slocum called. "Dingo, you better come on back, now."

Dingo made no move. Slocum jacked another shell into the chamber.

"Come on back," he called. "Or I'll shoot you in your other leg."

"No, no!" Dingo said, rising to a sitting position. "Don't shoot me again."

"Come on back."

"I can't," Dingo said. "I can't walk."

"Then crawl," Slocum ordered. "But do it now, or you'll be crawling on two crippled legs." He raised the rifle to his shoulder.

"No, no, wait," Dingo said. Slowly, painfully, he got up, then started limping back toward Slocum and the others. He pulled himself back up the side of the hill, then a short while later, was in front of them.

"Climb into the wagon," Slocum ordered. "All of you," he added.

Slocum made each of the three outlaws put their hands behind their backs. Then, using narrow strips of rawhide, he bound them by the simple expedient of tying their thumbs together.

"Why didn't you kill me?" Dingo asked.

"Shooting is too good for a no-count bastard like you," Slocum said. "I want you to hang."

"Yeah?" Dingo replied with a smug smile. "Well, I don't have to tell you that I was close enough to the gallows once before to get a smell of sulfur. But as you recall, I didn't get hung then, and I ain't goin' to get hung this time. So, I wouldn't go sendin' out any invitations."

"Percy, you drive. Ladies, go over behind those rocks and take a few minutes to change clothes," Slocum said. "You'll ride their horses."

Danielle, Delilah, and Marie went over to change into trousers and shirts. O'Riley and the breed strained their necks looking toward the rocks, hoping to see the women undressed.

"Turn back this way or I'll knock your teeth down your throat," Percy said threateningly.

Quickly, O'Riley, and the breed responded to his order.

"Hey, Slocum. I need me some doctorin' done to my leg," Dingo said.

With his knife, Slocum cut off the bottom of Dingo's trousers. He saw the entry and exit wound of the bullet.

"The bullet's not there," he said. "But the wound is liable to fester up some before we get you back."

"Enough to kill him, or just enough to lose his leg?" Percy asked.

"Could be enough to kill him," Slocum admitted.

"You said you didn't want to kill me," Dingo reminded him. "You said you wanted to keep me alive so's you could watch me hang."

"That's what I said, all right."

"Well, iffen the wound festers and I die, you won't get to watch me hang. So, I reckon you ought to do somethin' about it."

"You got any ideas about treatin' it?" Percy asked.

"Yeah," Slocum replied. "Yeah, I got an idea."

Slocum walked over to one of the outlaws' horses and began looking through the saddlebag. He found what he was looking for just as Danielle and the other two women returned, now dressed for riding.

"What is it?" Danielle asked. "What are you doing?"

"I'm about to treat Dingo's wound," Slocum said, pulling out a small bag of salt.

Slocum walked back over to the wagon. "This'll prob'ly hurt some," he said. "But it'll stop the festerin'." He began pouring salt on Dingo's wound, then he rubbed it in. Dingo grimaced and turned white with the pain, but he hung on while Slocum finished his work.

"There," Slocum said. "That ought to take care of it."

Slocum saw then that the women were smiling, really smiling, when they climbed onto the horses.

Percy started to climb up to the driver's seat but Slocum held up his hand.

"Wait," Slcom said. "I need a little insurance."

Using a series of loops and slipknots, Slocum tied the three outlaws together by their necks.

"You can't tie us together like this," Dingo said. "What if the wagon was to hit a bad bounce and one of us would fall out? If that happened, it would break all our necks."

"Don't fall out," Slocum replied coldly.

Slocum mounted his own horse then, and they started away. Behind them, in front of the cabin, was the fresh mound over the grave of young Verity Dixon. Slocum turned in his saddle to look back at it, and thought of the diary the young girl had written. He thought, also, of the Caulders, the young Peabody boy, and the horror these men had visited upon the young Peabody girl and her parents. As he thought about it, his blood ran cold, and he had to check the impulse to shoot all three of them.

They proceeded in silence for several minutes, then, following the path of a stream, rounded a bend so that the house was no longer visible. They started down a long, rock-strew slope.

"You men better hold on tight here," Slocum said. "I wouldn't want one of you to fall out."

"How we goin' to hold on? You got our hands tied behind out backs."

"You'll figure out a way."

"This ain't right, Slocum," Dingo complained.

"What's not right?"

"Loopin' us all together like this. Why don't you just keep us covered with your pistol?"

"I like the rope," Slocum said. "Look at it this way, Dingo. You were born for the rope."

"I don't mind getting shot," Dingo protested. "I just don't want my neck broke."

"You don't want your neck broke, huh?" Delilah asked. "Well, what do you think is going to happen to you when we turn you over to the law?"

"You ain't got us to the law yet," Dingo said. "And I figure you ain't goin' to."

"What makes you figure that?"

"I figure we're goin' to get Slocum here so pissed off, he'll go ahead and shoot us," Dingo said. He chuckled. "Ain't that about what you're figurin', O'Riley?"

"Yeah," O'Riley said.

" 'Course, being the law-abidin' citizen you are, it's goin' to pain you somewhat to shoot us like that," Dingo said. "But I reckon that's what's goin' to happen."

"I'm not going to shoot you," Slocum said.

"Yeah? You don't sound none too convincing to me," Dingo replied. "I seen the way you was lookin' at us when you was buryin' that little girl we killed. But, you just seen our bad side. If you had been here a few hours earlier, you would'a seen that we treated that little girl good. Real good, if you know what I mean?" Dingo made a couple of forward thrusts with his pelvis, then laughed out loud. The others laughed with him.

"Shut up, you foul-mouthed sonofabitch!" Slocum shouted. He drew his pistol and aimed it at Dingo's forehead. He pulled the hammer back and the cylinder rotated.

"Yes!" Dingo said. To the degree possible, he thrust his head forward, offering his forehead as a target. "Yes! Do it! Do it!"

Slocum wanted to kill this monster with every fiber of his being but, at the last minute, he managed to pull back.

"No," he said. "Not yet. That's too quick, too clean. You're going to hang."

• • •

After they were well under way, Danielle moved up to ride alongside Slocum.

"Do you really think they will hang?" she asked.

"Can you think of one reason why they shouldn't?" Slocum replied.

"*Non, monsieur,* I cannot think of any reason why they shouldn't hang. But I can think of many reasons why they may not hang."

"Dingo is under a sentence to be hanged, and there's no way a judge isn't going to sentence the other two bastards to the gallows as well."

"Dingo was sentenced to hang once before and got away. How do we know it won't happen again?"

Slocum looked over at the three outlaws, sitting in the back of the wagon. They were as unmoving as possible, sitting very carefully in order to keep from tightening the nooses around their necks.

"Don't worry about that," he said. "I give you my personal guarantee that Dingo will hang."

They stopped at high noon where they made a cold camp. Lunch was jerky and water. Dingo complained. He told Slocum that, as prisoners, they were entitled to be fed more than a strip of dried beef and a few sips of water each.

"That would be true, if you were prisoners of the law," Slocum said. "But you aren't prisoners of the law. You are my prisoners."

"What are you going to do with us?"

"Dingo," Slocum said, "if I had my way, I'd just throw the three of you in a cell somewhere. I would give you water, but no food, and I'd let the townsfolk come down to the jail each day, just to watch you die. Then, when you died, I'd throw you out in the back alley, like so much garbage, and let the dogs and pigs feed on your carcasses. So don't be complaining about what we're giving you to eat. Just be thankful you're getting anything at all."

It was late that afternoon before Dingo started talking, bragging about some of his exploits. Slocum knew what he was doing, knew he was trying to goad him into helping them escape the rope, even if that escape meant dying by bullet.

"O'Riley, did I ever tell how come they was wantin' to hang me 'n' ole Flatnose back there in Pinedale?" Dingo asked. Then, without giving O'Riley a chance to answer, he continued.

"We was workin' some for Ned Caulder, brandin' calves. See, we know'd he was about to sell 'em all, and when he done that, we planned to take his money. Which is what we done. But, a'fore we took his money, we had us a little fun with his woman. Turns out, Caulder's ole lady used to be a whore, so we figured, what the hell, it wouldn't be nothin' she'd never done before, right? Only, she didn't want nothin' to do with us."

"Who would want anything to do with you?" Delilah asked. "I'm a whore, and if you brought a thousand dollars to the house where I worked, I wouldn't have anything to do with you."

"Ha!" Dingo said. "Then you ain't no different from Caulder's whore. Except, she didn't have no say in the matter. Me 'n' Flatnose wouldn't take no for an answer, if you get my meanin'," he added with an evil laugh. "And, let me tell you, she was fine, too. Yes, sir, she was mighty, mighty fine."

"Shut up, you bastard!" Delilah said. She pulled a pistol from her holster, pointed it at him, and cocked it.

"No, Delilah, don't!" Slocum shouted. "Can't you see that's exactly what he wants?"

"Yeah? Well, I'm the one that can give him exactly what he wants," Delilah said sullenly. Reluctantly, she put her pistol away.

"Haven't heard enough yet, huh?" Dingo asked. "Say, O'Riley, you recollect that wagon we stopped three, maybe four months ago? The one with the woman that just had a baby?"

"Yeah," O'Riley said. "Yeah, I do recollect that." O'Riley laughed. "That's the time when we tied the woman to her husband so's he could be right there when we showed her what a real man could do for her."

"You know, I almost hated to kill them," Dingo said. "If it hadn't of been so much trouble to take 'em along, I would'a let them live."

"You killed them?" Marie asked. "Are you saying you killed an entire family?"

"Not the entire family," O'Riley said. "We left one of 'em alive."

"Yeah, we didn't kill the baby," Dingo said.

"What happened to the baby?" Marie asked.

O'Riley laughed. "Well, the baby was needin' a tit to suck on, and wasn't none of us equipped to take care of it, if you know what I mean."

"What did you do with the baby?" Marie asked again.

"What the hell do you think we did with him? We just left him there, lyin' in the wagon alongside his mama and daddy. Don't know what happened to him after that."

"I have never encountered more degenerate filth than you three men," Delilah said.

"I liked the nuns," Pablo said. It was the first time the breed had spoken since they had been put into the wagon.

Dingo laughed. "Yeah, they was good. But it's been near a whole year since we had them. You still thinkin' about them?"

"Was good," Pablo said.

"Nuns?" Danielle said, nearly choking in her anger. "You raped some nuns?"

"There was three of 'em as I recollect," Dingo said. "Only, one of 'em was so old and drawed-up ugly, that we shot her right away. The other two we took to our camp and tied 'em up side by side."

"We kept 'em for three days," O'Riley went on. "The whole time we had them, they was prayin' an' callin' to Jesus."

Dingo laughed. "You should'a seen the breed. He went from one to another, back and forth, back and forth."

"You know, the thing is," O'Riley said, "I always had it in my mind that them two nuns was a'likin' what we was doin' for them. You know, nuns, they don't have no men around, so, you gotta know they get to wantin' it ever now and then."

"You 'member what that one said just before you cut her throat, Breed?" O'Riley asked. "She said she forgave us."

"Yeah," Dingo said. "I guess that plumb riled me more'n anything. That pious bitch tellin' us she forgave us."

"You bastards!" Percy suddenly shouted. Turning around in his seat, he grabbed the breed's foot and jerked it up, causing Pablo to tumble over the side of the wagon. The other two outlaws, seeing the breed go over, had to throw themselves out of the wagon as well to keep their necks from being broken. With the three men lying in the dirt, Percy jumped down from the wagon and began pummeling the three men, first one, then the other. The ropes tightened around their necks.

"Pull him off! Pull him off!" Dingo shouted, his voice, high-pitched with terror.

Slocum stopped, then swung down from his horse as slowly and deliberately as if he were dismounting in front of a general store. He handed his reins to Danielle, then walked over to where Percy was working over O'Riley.

"That's enough," Slocum said, calmly. "Get back up on the wagon."

Percy snorted, kicked O'Riley one last time, square in the crotch, then climbed back into the wagon. O'Riley doubled over while Dingo and Pablo gagged as the nooses tightened around their necks, uncomfortable, but no longer in danger of having their necks broken.

16

"We may as well camp here," Slocum said, when they stopped again, near sundown. He looked around. "That's a nice cottonwood grove, we can find some firewood in there. And over there's the Sweetwater River for water."

"We covered some ground today," Percy said.

"What do you think, John? About two more days back to Pinedale?" Danielle asked.

"About two days," Slocum agreed. "Percy, you take care of the horses. Danielle, you and the other ladies can get our supper started."

Percy began hobbling the horses while the women got some bacon, beans, and coffee from the saddlebags. Marie started carving off thick pieces of meat.

"You got no right to let Percy work us over like he done," Dingo said, still rankling over the events at the noon stop. "He could'a beat us to death, and you wasn't doin' nothn' to stop him."

"I should'a let him beat all three of you to death," Slocum said.

149

"We're your prisoners," Dingo said. "According to the law, you got to treat us square."

"I told you once before, this doesn't have anything to do with the law," Slocum said.

"What do you mean it don't have nothin' to do with the law? You was with Morgan when me and Flatnose was picked up. Are you tryin' to tell us you didn't have nothin' to do with the law then?"

"I didn't have nothin' to do with the law then, and I don't have anything to do with it now."

Dingo looked confused. "Then, I don't understand. What are you doin' here? What'd you come after us for? Are you after the reward?"

"I don't care about the reward."

"Then what? I don't understand. Explain it to me, if you will."

"I'm sure I couldn't explain."

"Try."

"All right. I came to see justice done," Slocum said.

"Justice? You? Don't make me laugh," Dingo said. He looked toward Percy, who was now coming back after having staked out the horses. "What about ole Percy there? How come you ain't bringin' him in? He used to ride with us. Now he's turned on his own kind."

"Don't call me your own kind," Percy said with a growl. "I've done some bad things in my day, but I ain't never done the evil you have done."

"Ahh, enough of all this," Dingo said. "You didn't hardly feed us nothin' a'tall at noon and I'm getting hungry. I'm ready for my supper."

"*Mon dieu*, how can you talk about eating after the stories you have told us?" Danielle asked. Danielle had found a log to sit on and was holding her head as if she was going to be sick.

"What's one got to do with the other?" Dingo asked. "Killin's killin', an' eatin's eatin'."

"Are you all right, Danielle?" Slocum asked.

"As God is my witness, I have never encountered Satan's angels, before, but there is a smell of sulfur about these men. I intend to dance a jig as the ropes tighten around the necks of these evil ones."

Percy came back into the camp with an armload of firewood. He laid the wood for the fire, then lit it. A moment later flames danced and leaped against the circle of rocks he had constructed. Marie lay five slices of bacon in one pan, then opened a couple of cans of beans and put them in another. Delilah hung a coffeepot from a hooked limb.

"There's only five pieces of meat in that pan," Dingo pointed out. "But there's eight of us."

"This is our meat, not yours," Slocum said.

"What the hell are you talkin' about? You gotta feed us."

"You're right," Slocum said. Dingo grinned triumphantly as Slocum began untying their thumbs, so they could use their hands. A moment later the grin faded when he saw Slocum unwrap some jerky. Slocum threw a piece of jerky to each of the prisoners.

"What the hell is this?" Dingo demanded. "You expect us to eat this while you're eatin' bacon and beans?"

"And biscuits," Marie said with a smile. She looked pointedly at the prisoners. "For us," she added. "Not for you."

"You don't have to eat the jerky," Slocum said. "You can go without. You won't be living long enough to starve to death."

A few minutes later, Percy came over to sit on a log

near Slocum. "You want my bacon?" he asked. "I ain't touched it none."

"You don't like bacon?"

Percy shook his head. "It ain't that I don't like it," he said. "It's just that . . . well, since I quit drinkin', I can't hardly hold nothin' down. Which is okay, 'cause I ain't never been that much of a eater anyway. And right now I'm only hungry for one thing, and that's whiskey."

"You'll get over that," Slocum said. "And you'll be a lot better man when you do. You're a lot better man now."

Percy smiled. "You know, I reckon that's true, ain't it?" He got up, poured himself a cup of coffee, then brought the pot around and poured for each of the women. He stopped right in the middle and looked at the hand that was holding the coffeepot. His smile grew broader. "Look," he said. "No shakes." He went back to sit beside Slocum again.

"You're doin' fine, Percy," Slocum said. "You're going to make it."

"I am going to make it," Percy replied. "Listen, Slocum, I'm sorry about goin' a little out of control a while back, and attackin' them men like I done," he said. "But listenin' to them tell about the rapin' and killin', and thinkin' 'bout what they done to that little girl back there, I just couldn't take it no more. To think that I ever rode with the likes of these sonsofbitches."

"John, I'm about the same way," Delilah said. "I just don't know if I can stomach another day with these bastards. They are worse than rattlesnakes. A rattlesnake is only doing what nature intended it to do. I can't believe nature intended men like this to live."

"You've been around such men before, John," Marie said. "Have you seen many like this?"

Slocum took a swallow of his coffee before he answered.

"I have been around outlaws before, and I've faced them down in gunfights. Some of the men I've killed even had a sense of honor, in their own way. And others I've run across would press a man hard to find any good to them at all. But, in all the men I've come across, I don't believe I have ever run into anyone like these men."

"Slocum, you remember a man by the name of Arnie Spitzen? He robbed a bank up near Denver."

"Spitzen? Yes, I remember him."

"I was deputyin' some then. Spitzen killed three people when he robbed that bank. He killed a teller, a guard, and a woman who just happened to be there. He got away and was holed up in a cave when we caught up with him. He said we'd never take him alive, and we didn't."

"You were once a deputy, *Monsieur* Keith?" Marie asked, surprised at Percy's revelation.

"More'n once," Percy said.

"I thought you were an outlaw."

Percy chuckled. "Ma'am, I've rode on both sides of the law. And I ain't the only one of my kind to do that."

"That's true," Slocum said. "Often, out here, the line between law breaking and law enforcing is razor thin."

"Anyhow, Slocum, what I'm getting to," Percy said, continuing his story, "is the fact we didn't have no intention to take him alive. You see, the woman he killed in the bank was the woman the marshal had set his sites to marry. We set out to kill Spitzen, and that's just what we done."

"You've got something in your craw, Percy," Slocum said, studying the man across the cup of his coffee. "What is it?"

Percy looked over at Dingo and the others. "Let's kill

these bastards," he said. "Hell, Dingo's already been sentenced to die, we wouldn't be doin' nothin' but carryin' out the Judge's orders."

"What about the other two?"

"Maybe you don't know this, but there's paper out on them, wanted, dead or alive. They'd be a lot easier packin' back in dead, than alive. And because of the paper saying they're wanted dead or alive, there wouldn't be no questions asked if we was to bring 'em back dead."

"I think *Monsieur* Keith has a point," Delilah said. "Look at them over there. They're still talking and laughing about all the killing and raping they've done. I'm sick of it."

"They're trying to goad us into shooting them," Slocum said. "Can't you see that?"

"I say, let them succeed," Marie said. "I think we ought to put a bullet in their brains right now."

"*Mon chere*, what makes you think they have any brains?" Danielle asked, and the others laughed.

Slocum tossed out the coffee grounds that were in the bottom of his cup, then he stood and walked over to where the three prisoners were tied.

"I've got to piss," Dingo said. "Send one of those sweet things over here to hold my cock for me while I piss." He laughed, and the others laughed with him.

Slocum pulled his pistol and pointed it at Dingo.

"So, you're going to shoot me, are you?" Dingo asked. He closed his eyes. "Well, do it then. Do it and to hell with you."

Slocum cocked his pistol and the cylinder rolled, then locked into place. He lined the sights up on Dingo's forehead. Dingo snickered.

"Like the little nun said, Slocum, I forgive you," Dingo said.

Suddenly a hot fury passed over Slocum. A fury that couldn't be satisfied by a quick, easy bullet. He let the hammer down, then, with a loud curse, slammed the gun back into his holster.

"Shoot, you coward!" Dingo shouted. "Shoot me, you son of a bitch!"

Slocum smiled at him. "No, I'm not going to shoot you. I said you were going to hang, and that is exactly what you are going to do."

"Oh yeah? We'll see about that," Dingo taunted as Slocum walked over to the others. "You seen what happened last time they tried."

17

Through the long, last, two hours of his watch, John Slocum sat with his back to a rock, watching the glowing coals of the small campfire. To his right, Percy and the three women breathed softly as they lay wrapped in their bedrolls. Down from the knoll on a sandy flat, slept the three outlaws, securely tied to a Joshua tree. Because they had used Dingo's blanket and poncho to bury the little girl, he was lying on the bare ground. It had gotten a bit brisk during the night, and the outlaw was now lying in a fetal position trying to find some warmth. He, and the other two were snoring.

The fact that all three outlaws were sleeping peacefully, snoring away without the slightest twinge of conscience, began to get to Slocum. How could anyone be so callous as to be able to cut a young girl's throat, then be able to enjoy the sleep of the innocent?

Slocum felt the bile of anger rising in his throat. It was all he could do to keep from killing these bastards where they lay. But that would really be letting them off easy. If he killed them while they were sleeping, they'd never experience any of the fear they had caused in so many others.

In the east, a streak of red preceded the sunrise and Slocum watched as the top curve of the sun began to peek just above the horizon. A doe came out from a stand of aspens and stood quietly, sniffing the wind. Because it was upwind from Slocum and the others, it didn't smell any danger, but still, it hesitated.

Slocum watched the deer, and thought about how good a roast of venison would taste. He moved slowly, quietly, toward his saddle, then, bending over, still undetected by the deer, slipped his Winchester from its sheath. Very slowly, and quietly, he jacked a round into the chamber, then aimed at the deer.

The deer, still not perceiving any danger, moved down to the edge of the river. Once again the deer looked around. Slocum eased back on the hammer and slowly began to squeeze the trigger. Just before he fired, he caught something in the corner of his eye. A yearling slipped out of the woods then, and hurried down to the water to drink beside its mother.

Slocum watched the two deer for a moment, drinking side by side, then he realized that even the prospect of fresh meat wasn't enough to make him want to shoot. He lowered his rifle.

"Go ahead, critters," he said under his breath. "Drink your water in peace. I'm not going to shoot you."

After the deer drank their fill, they disappeared back into the woods. In the river, a fish jumped. Whatever exuberance caused the fish to jump was fatal, because almost immediately thereafter, an eagle swooped down, reached into the water with its claws, then climbed back into the air, clutching the struggling fish in its talons.

The deer, the fish, the eagle, even the beautiful sunrise,

were all a part of nature. There was a natural order to things, but from time to time, something, or someone, would upset that natural order. People like Dingo, O'Riley, and the breed, had upset the natural order. And when something like that happened it was necessary for things to be put right again.

Suddenly, Slocum knew what he was going to do. Walking back to where Percy and the three women were sleeping, he kicked them, gently, on the bottom of their feet.

"Wake up," he said. "Wake up, all of you. We've got work to do."

Groggily the others began to awaken.

"Let's go," he said. "Time's wasting. We have a town to charter."

Danielle was the first one up, and she stretched, then rubbed her eyes. For a moment she just stared off into space while coming fully conscious. Then, as if suddenly realizing what Slocum had just said, she looked toward him with a puzzled expression on her face.

"I beg your pardon," she said. "What did you just say? Something about a town?"

"I said we have a town to charter," Slocum replied easily.

"What town?"

"The town of Verity. Verity, Wyoming."

"John Slocum, you aren't making a bit of sense," Danielle said.

By now the others were awake enough to follow the conversation, though they were as puzzled by Slocum's strange remarks as was Danielle.

"What are you talking about?" Marie asked. "What do you mean, we have a town to build?"

"Not build, charter."

"How can you charter a town without building it first?"

"Do you think a town is made just of buildings? Houses, stores, saloons, and such?" Slocum asked.

"No, of course not, but . . ."

"Before the houses, stores, and buildings, there are the people. Towns are made up of people," Slocum insisted. "And people, we have. There are eight of us here. I've been in towns that were smaller."

"Eight?"

"Yes, counting them," Slocum said, pointing toward the three outlaws, who were also just beginning to awaken.

"Well, if we really were going to start a town, I sure wouldn't want those people in it," Delilah said.

"Oh, but they have to be in it," Slocum replied mysteriously. "That's the whole point of it, don't you see?"

Although the outlaws had been tied, not only to the Joshua tree, but ankle to ankle as well, their hands weren't tied and Dingo, who was now awake and on his feet, began to relieve himself in full view of the women.

"You could at least turn your back, you son of a bitch!" Marie called over to him. "You are disgusting!"

"You're a whore," Dingo called back. "It ain't like you've never seen a cock before." He laughed, and the other two outlaws laughed with him.

"Ohhh!" Marie said angrily. Then, to Slocum, "How could you even think of including them in any town you might start? Especially a town named Verity, after that sweet young girl they murdered."

"Oh, the town has to be called Verity," Slocum replied. "It's only fitting, that the town that tries, convicts, and executes these three men, be named for her."

"What?" Percy asked, his interest suddenly awakened. "Slocum, what do you have in mind?"

"I told you. I have in mind starting the town of Verity,"

Slocum said. "Once we are incorporated, we will elect a marshal, a mayor, and a judge."

"You're serious, aren't you?" Marie asked.

"I've never been more serious in my life," Slocum replied. "Percy, get those three men over here."

Percy walked down the little rise to the place where the three men had been tied, then brought them back to where Slocum and the women waited.

"Sit down," Slocum said.

"I've been on the ground all night. I prefer to stand," Dingo replied.

"Sit them down, Percy," Slocum said.

Percy jerked on the rope that was tied to their ankles. As a result, the three outlaws went down hard.

"Hey, that hurt!" Dingo complained. "I've got a shot-up leg, don't forget."

"Be quiet," Slocum ordered. "The meeting is about to come to order."

"What meeting?" Dingo asked.

"I hereby call this meeting to order," Slocum said, making no effort to answer Dingo's question. "Marie, do you still have the ledger book Verity was keeping as a diary?"

"Yes," Marie answered.

"And a pencil?"

"Yes."

"Good, then you are hereby appointed as secretary. In order for everything to be on the up-and-up, I want you to write down everything that we say or do, from now on."

"Minutes," Danielle said.

"What?"

"It's called keeping the minutes," Danielle explained with a smile.

"Yeah," Slocum said. "That will make it official. Marie, you keep the minutes."

"All right," Marie agreed.

"What's all this about?" Dingo asked. He didn't understand what was going on, and he was clearly discomfited by it.

"The purpose of this meeting is to incorporate the town of Verity," Slocum began. "The town we incorporate will be named after the young girl who was murdered by these three men. All in favor of the incorporation of the town of Verity, raise your right hand."

Percy and the three women raised their hands. Then, Slocum put up his own hand.

"Anyone against incorporating the town?" Slocum asked. He looked at Dingo and the other two. "Are you three men going to vote for, or against incorporation?"

"You mean we have a vote?"

"The population of the town, once it is incorporated, will be eight," Slocum said. "That number includes you three men. So I ask you now: Do you intend to vote?"

"I ain't never voted for anything in my life," Dingo said. "Why should I vote now?" He laughed.

"Because once we are incorporated as a town, I intend to convene a court, and try the three of you for murder," Slocum said. "And after we find you guilty, I intend to hang you."

The smile left Dingo's face. "What? What are you talking about, you are going to try us for murder? You can't do that. It's illegal."

"As an incorporated town, we will make our own laws," Slocum said. "Therefore anything we do will be legal, simply because we choose to do it. Now, I ask you again. How do you vote? Are you in favor of incorporation, or opposed?"

"I'm against it," Dingo said. He looked at the other two. "We're all against it."

"Marie, let the record show that the town of Verity was incorporated by a vote of five to three."

"Right," Marie said.

"Wait a minute!" Dingo said. "That ain't right. The vote was three to two against startin' up a town."

"Three to two? How did you come up with that number?" Slocum asked.

Dingo smiled broadly. "It was us three against you and Percy. I reckon you didn't count on that, did you?"

"There are five of us," Slocum replied.

"That's only if you count the women's votes," Dingo said smugly.

"I *am* counting their votes."

"Women can't vote," Dingo said.

"Yeah, women can't vote," O'Riley added, and the three outlaws began congratulating themselves.

"Sorry, Dingo, but you had the misfortune to perpetrate your evil deeds in Wyoming," Delilah said, simply.

"So, we're in Wyoming. What does that mean?" Dingo asked.

"It means you should be a little more civic-minded," Delilah replied. "Maybe if you were, you would know that in Wyoming, women have the vote."

"What? Women can vote in Wyoming? Why, I've never heard of such a thing."

"We can vote, hold office, and serve on juries," Delilah said triumphantly.

"Now that we are a town, the first item of official business will be to elect a judge," Slocum said. "And I aim to put myself up for that position."

"I second the nomination," Marie said.

"Any other nominations?"

"Yeah," Dingo said quickly. "I nominate myself."

"Any seconds?"

"O'Riley seconds the nomination," Dingo said.

"That doesn't count. He has to say it."

"Say it," Dingo said.

"Why? I might want to be the judge my ownself," O'Riley said.

"Say it, you son of a bitch!" Dingo ordered.

"All right," O'Riley said reluctantly. "I second it."

The vote was held, and Slocum was elected judge of the town of Verity, Wyoming, by a vote of five to three. Percy was elected marshal and Danielle was elected mayor, by the same five to three vote.

"Marie, do you have all that recorded in your book?" Slocum asked.

"Yes."

"Good. Now, I want you to record that as duly elected judge in and for the town of Verity, Wyoming, I am issuing a warrant for the arrest of Angus Dingo, Pablo Goxando, and Kelly O'Riley. They are being charged with the murder of Verity Dixon."

"What about Kathy Caulder?" Danielle asked. "I mean, that's the whole reason we are here. Seems to me like it would be a shame to come this far, and not have it be for her."

"I agree," Marie said.

"Wait a minute, me and the breed didn't have nothin' to do with killin' anyone named Kathy Caulder," O'Riley said.

"Add to Dingo, the charge of the murder of Ned and Kathy Caulder," Slocum said.

Nodding, Marie continued to write.

"Danielle, in addition to being the mayor, I'm appointing you as the prosecutor. Do you think you are up to it?"

"Oui, monsieur," Danielle said. "I can prosecute them."

"Delilah, I want you to defend them."

"Me?" Delilah replied. "Why me? I don't want to defend them. I want to see the bastards hang."

"Because I know you are smart enough to do a good job," Slocum said. "And, Delilah, I want you to do the best job you can. Otherwise, this won't be a trial, this will be a lynching. And if we lynch them, we are no better than they are. Do you understand?"

"I understand what you are saying, but I don't see how I can defend them. I saw them kill the little Dixon girl, and I heard Dingo bragging about killing Kathy. So I know they are guilty. It's not possible for a lawyer to defend people if she knows they are guilty, is it?" Delilah asked.

"*Oui*, it is possible," Danielle said. "All the law requires is that the defendants are provided with counsel. There is nothing that says a lawyer must believe in the innocence of his client."

"Is that a fact? Or are you just saying that?" Percy asked.

"No. That is a fact," Danielle replied.

"How do you know so much about law?"

"*Monsieur* Keith, have you ever been to New Orleans?" Danielle replied, sweetly.

"No, I can't say as I have."

"Well, if you had, you would no doubt have heard of a man named Phillipe Garneau. He is the most prominent attorney of that city."

"And you know him?" Slocum asked.

"Knew him? *Monsieur* Slocum, I am married to him," Danielle answered.

"Danielle, I never knew you were married," Marie said.

Danielle paused for a moment, then sighed. "Phillipe is a very good man, from a fine, old, New Orleans family.

I, on the other hand, am an octoroon, bred for but one purpose. When his family learned of my background, they insisted that Phillipe have the marriage annulled."

"And did he?" Marie asked. "No, wait, you said you *are* married to him, not that you *were* married. Does that mean you are still married?"

"I really don't know. Phillipe did not want to annul the marriage," Danielle said. "He knew where I came from." She smiled. "In fact, he was our best customer. But, to spare him any further pain or humiliation, I decided to leave New Orleans. I'm sure that, by now, the marriage has been annulled. But, as I have never seen any papers to that effect, I choose to consider myself as still married."

"So, while you were with him, you picked up a little law, did you?" Percy asked.

"Yes. As his wife, I kept his records, and helped him prepare his cases. Phillipe often said that had it not been for the fact that women could not stand before the bar, I would have made a fine lawyer."

"Well, you are going to get your chance to do that today," Slocum said.

"What about me?" Delilah asked. "I don't know anything at all about the law."

"Maybe not. But I know you well enough now to know that you have intelligence and common sense. That's a very good combination to have and if it came right down to it, I'd rather have you as my lawyer than many an educated counselor I've known."

"That's the truth," Danielle said. Smiling, she put her hand on her friend's shoulder. "Don't worry about it, Delilah, you'll do fine."

"Marie, you will be the court clerk. It's very important you keep notes of everything that happens."

"All right," Marie agreed.

"And, Percy, as the town marshal, I want you to also act as the bailiff."

"I'll do it," Percy agreed.

"Good. That means we're ready to go."

"Wait a minute!" Dingo said. "You can't do this!"

"Oh but we can, and we are doing it," Slocum answered.

"What about a jury?" Dingo pointed to the others. "You've given each one of them a job to do, but there's no one left to be the jury."

"We'll have a jury of one," Slocum replied.

"One? And who will that one person be?" Dingo asked.

"Me," Slocum answered. "I will be judge, jury, and executioner."

"Executioner? What if the prosecutor doesn't make the case? Are you still going to execute us?"

"No," Slocum said.

Dingo grinned broadly. "Well now, that's more like it," he said. "We might just fool you. We might just be found innocent. Then what will you do?"

"Hang you," Slocum said easily.

"Hang us? Wait a minute! I thought you just said you wouldn't execute us if we were found not guilty."

"If you are found not guilty, and I hang you, I would call it murder, not execution. But whatever it is called, believe me when I tell you this, Angus Dingo. Before the sun goes down tonight, you and these two miserable bastards who chose to run with you will be hanging from that cottonwood tree." Slocum pointed to a large cottonwood that stood on the banks of the river. About ten feet up the trunk of the tree, a large arm protruded parallel with the ground, making it a perfect crossbar for the hangman's ropes.

Dingo blanched, visibly. It was his first real show of fear since he had been captured.

"Bailiff," Slocum said. "Call the court to session."

18

"Hear ye, hear ye, hear ye!" Percy called in his most sten-torian voice. "This here court of Verity in Sweetwater County, Wyoming, is in session." He paused, then looked over at Danielle. "They always say something else after that," he said.

"The Honorable John Slocum presiding," Danielle suggested.

"Yeah, that's it. I know'd it was somethin' like that. The Honorable John Slocum presiding," he added.

Slocum, who was sitting on a large log, looked over toward the three sullen-faced prisoners.

"Angus Dingo, Kelly O'Riley, and Pablo Goxando, you are charged with the rape and murder of Verity Dixon. Angus Dingo, you are also charged with the rape and murder of Kathy Caulder. How do you plead?"

"We ain't pleadin' nothin'," Dingo said, "seein' as how this ain't no real court."

"This is as real a court as you are going to see," Slocum said. "Now, how do you plead?"

"Uh, John, can I object to something?" Delilah asked.

167

"You should address him as Your Honor," Danielle suggested.

Delilah giggled. "For crying out loud, Danielle, I've slept with the man," she said. "It's kind of hard to think of him as Your Honor after that."

"If this court is to be real, we must follow all the rules," Danielle said. "Address him as Your Honor. And if you want to object, just say 'I object.' You don't have to have his permission. He can sustain or overrule the objection, but you can object anytime you want."

"All right," Delilah agreed. "Your Honor, I object."

"What are you objecting to?" Slocum asked.

"When you told Percy to put these men under arrest, you said you were arresting them for murder. You didn't say anything about rape. I don't think they are being charged with rape."

Slocum thought for a moment, then he nodded. "All right," he said. "Objection is sustained." He looked at the prisoners. "You men aren't being charged with rape, just with murder in the first degree. Now, how do you plead?"

"I told you, we ain't pleadin' nothin'," Dingo insisted.

"Very well, Counselor, you enter a plea for them."

"Before I do that, I'd like to ask Danielle something, if I may."

"You may," Slocum said.

"Danielle, you know all about this. Tell me what murder in the first degree is," Delilah said.

"Murder in first degree means premeditated murder," Danielle explained. "That means you plan it, and then you do it. Also, there is no set length of time between when you plan it and when you do it. From the idea to the actual murder could be as quick as thought, and still be murder in the first degree."

"What if somebody is crazy? Isn't there something

about people being found not guilty because they are crazy?"

"Wait a minute here! Are you saying we're crazy?" Dingo shouted angrily.

"Bailiff, silence the prisoner," Slocum said.

"Yes, sir!" Percy replied. Stepping over to the place where the three prisoners stood, tied together, Percy backhanded Dingo hard, across the face. "Shut up, you bastard," he said with a low, menacing growl.

Percy's face turned red where Dingo had hit him.

"If somebody is crazy, then he can't be found guilty of first-degree murder," Danielle said, answering Delilah's question.

"Why not?"

"Because if he is crazy, he don't really have a concept of what is right and what is wrong. If he don't understand the difference between right and wrong, then society cannot hold him responsible for committing a wrong."

"Does that answer your question?" Slocum asked.

"Yes, it does," Delilah said. Then, as an afterthought, she added, "Your Honor."

"Are you now ready to answer my question as to how your clients plead?"

"They plead not guilty," Delilah said.

"Not guilty. Did you hear that?" Dingo asked the other two defendants. "Hot damn, maybe this girl knows what she is doing after all."

"Are you saying they are not guilty because they didn't do it?" Slocum asked.

Delilah shook her head. "No. They did it. We all saw them do it."

"Hold on here!" Dingo said. "I thought you was supposed to be defendin' us."

"But, according to what Danielle said, if someone is

crazy and he does something, well, he isn't guilty because he is crazy."

"The correct plea would be not guilty, and not guilty by reason of insanity," Danielle explained.

"All right," Slocum said. "The plea is not guilty, and, not guilty by reason of insanity. Prosecutor, you may make your case."

Danielle had been sitting on a rock and she stood up and dusted off the seat of her pants. Slocum had not known that Danielle was an octoroon until she told them about herself, and now as he looked more closely at her, he could see the golden hue to her skin, the deep, brown eyes, and the dark, almost blue-black hair. Whatever her background, Danielle was a strikingly beautiful woman who would be at home in the finest mansions in America. That she was standing on the pebble-strewn bank of the Sweetwater River in the wilds of Wyoming, arguing a case before this impromptu court, made the situation seem all the more bizarre.

"Your Honor, prosecution intends to prove that these three defendants did indeed murder Verity Dixon. In addition, prosecution will prove that Angus Dingo also murdered Kathy Caulder. And now, if I may, I would like to call my first witness."

"Go ahead," Slocum said.

"Prosecution calls Percy Keith."

"Percy, you can sit on the end of the log there," Slocum said, pointing to the other end of the same log he was occupying.

"Thanks," Percy said, sitting where directed.

"Raise your right hand," Slocum ordered. When Percy did so, Slocum went on. "Do you swear to tell the truth, the whole truth, and nothing but the truth?"

"Yeah, I'll do that," Percy said.

"Prosecution may begin."

Danielle walked over to stand in front of Percy. "*Monsieur* Keith, did you lead us to the cabin where we found these three men?"

"Yes, Your Honor," Percy replied.

Danielle smiled. "You don't have to 'Your Honor' me, just the judge. But it does sound nice."

The others laughed.

"Yes, I led you folks to the cabin," Percy said.

"And what did we find, when we got there?"

"We found them three men," Percy said, pointing to the defendants.

"Was anyone else there?"

"Yeah, the little girl, Verity Dixon, was there."

"Was she alive?"

"She was alive when we got there."

"What happened to her?"

"O'Riley cut her throat," Percy said.

"Wait a minute!" O'Riley yelled. "It was Dingo's idea. He's the one made me do it!"

"Be quiet, O'Riley. You'll get your turn to talk," Slocum said.

"And, did you hear Dingo confess to the murder of Kathy Caulder?" Danielle continued.

"Yeah, I heard him bragging about that."

"I have no further questions, Your Honor."

"I have a question," Delilah said.

"Go ahead," Slocum replied.

"Percy." Delilah stopped then looked around. "Is it all right if I call him Percy?"

"Court has no objections," Slocum replied.

"Percy, when O'Riley cut Verity's throat, were you looking at him?"

"Yes, ma'am, I was," O'Riley replied. "I was looking right at him."

"Did he know you were looking at him?"

"Yes, ma'am, he did."

"In fact, he knew that all of us were looking right at him, didn't he?"

"Yes, ma'am, I reckon he did."

"But he cut her throat anyway, even knowing that every one of us were watching him."

"Yes, ma'am, he done it just as cool as a cucumber."

"As cool as a cucumber. All right, thank you. Oh, and one more question. When you heard Dingo say he had killed Kathy, did you think it was a confession? Or did you think he was bragging?"

"Well, he was sort of bragging about it, but—"

"Thank you, no more questions," Delilah said, interrupting Percy's answer.

Percy stopped in mid-sentence.

"You may step down," Slocum said.

Danielle called all the other witnesses in turn, including Slocum, who while he was a witness, gave witness testimony independent of his position as judge.

After Percy, Slocum, and Marie testified, Danielle called upon Delilah. To Slocum's surprise, Delilah stepped out of her role of defender of the three men and provided testimony every bit as damning as that provided by Percy Keith. And, like Percy Keith, she glared with hate and anger at the outlaws during her time on the witness stand.

When Danielle completed her direct examination of the witness, she turned to Slocum.

"Your Honor, I would now, normally turn my witness over to the defense counsel. But, as this *is* the defense counsel, I'm not certain as to the procedure."

"Your Honor, while I was testifying for the prosecution, I was the best witness I could be," Delilah said. "Now, I'll be the lawyer defending them again, and I'll do the best I can in that job."

"All right, you may continue," Slocum said.

Looking straight out from her seat on the far end of the log, and sitting up as straight as if she were in court back in Cheyenne, or even Denver, Delilah went on.

"I would ask myself these questions," Delilah said. "Was I looking right at O'Riley when he killed the little girl? The answer to that question is yes, I was. Did I think Dingo was actually making a confession when he talked about killing Kathy Caulder? No, I do not, because I don't think he thought of it as a confession. He was clearly bragging."

The questions did not surprise anyone anymore, because she had asked those same two questions of Percy, Marie, and Slocum.

"Any more questions?" Slocum asked Danielle.

"No, Your Honor. This concludes my case."

"All right, Delilah, you may begin your case," Slocum said.

"Your Honor, I call Angus Dingo to the stand."

Slocum signaled for Danielle to come over, then he asked both of them to step up to the log so he could talk to them quietly.

"What is it? What's wrong?" Delilah asked.

"Danielle, you know more about this than I do," Slocum said. "But seems to me I heard somewhere that a defendant doesn't have to testify if he doesn't want to. Is that true?"

"Yes," Danielle said. "The accused cannot be made to testify against himself."

"But sometimes they do?"

"If they waive that right. But, you must give them the opportunity to refuse."

"All right," Slocum said. He looked over at Dingo. "Your attorney has called you as a witness. You have the right to refuse to testify."

"Hell no, I'll testify," Dingo replied. "I've got a thing or two I want to tell this . . . so-called . . . court."

Slocum smiled. He had counted on Dingo's belligerence to make him want to testify. Now there would be no question as to whether or not he was given the opportunity not to incriminate himself.

"Do you swear to tell the truth, the whole truth, and nothing but the truth, so help you God?" Slocum asked.

"Yeah, well, me'n God ain't exactly on what you might call friendly terms," Dingo said. "But I reckon I'll tell you what you want to hear. Onliest thing is, I'm tied to the other two yahoos."

"No need. They can come over to the witness stand with you."

Moving awkwardly because of the way they were tied, the three men moved over to the end of the log that had been converted into the witness box.

"Mister Dingo," Delilah began, but her question was interrupted by laughter from O'Riley and Goxando. "Did I say something funny?" Delilah asked.

"You called Dingo 'Mister' " O'Riley said. "Don't think I've ever heard anyone call him 'Mister.' "

"There's a first time for everything, O'Riley," Slocum said. "Including a first time to die."

Slocum's observation wiped the smile from O'Riley's face, and he sat on the ground near the log, glaring as Delilah continued her cross-examination.

"Mister. Dingo," she said again. "How many men have you killed?"

"What? What kind of question is that?"

"It's a simple question. How many people have you killed?"

"I don't know. Killin' people is like takin' a piss. Who the hell keeps track of how many times you take a piss?"

"We're not talking about urinating, Mister Dingo. We're talking about killing. Now, how many people have you killed?"

"Fifteen, twenty, maybe," Dingo said. "Not countin' Mexicans or Indians."

"What do you mean, not counting them?"

"I don't count them."

"They are human beings."

"Not to me, they ain't."

"Pablo Goxando is half-Mexican and half-Indian. Do you feel that way about him as well? He is your friend."

"The breed? He ain't my friend."

"What do you mean, he isn't your friend? You ride with him."

"I ride with my horse, too. I don't call my horse my friend."

"Delilah, you're supposed to be defending this man," Slocum said. "Do you have a reason for asking this?"

"I'm through with this witness," Delilah said.

Danielle, surprised that Delilah turned the witness over so quickly, was slightly taken aback. Nevertheless, she recovered quickly, and walked over to stand in front of Dingo.

"Mister. Dingo, did you kill Verity Dixon?"

"No," Dingo said, smiling triumphantly. "O'Riley killed her. Hell, you all seen it. You done said that."

"You sonofabitch! You told me to do it!" O'Riley swore.

"Is that right? Did you tell O'Riley to kill the girl?"

"Well, yeah, I reckon I did. But I didn't do it myself."

"When you were bragging in the wagon, that you killed Kathy Caulder, was it bragging? Or was it fact?"

The smile on Dingo's face turned devious. "I ain't goin' to talk about that no more," he said.

"I have no further questions of this witness," Danielle said.

"Danielle, what do you call it when I want to ask him something else?" Delilah asked.

"Redirect," Danielle answered.

"All right, I have a redirect," Delilah said.

"Go ahead," Slocum said.

"Mister Dingo, when you knew we were looking right at you, as we are now, why did you have that girl killed? I mean, you had to know we were watching."

"Yeah, I know'd you was watchin'."

"And did you know that if we saw it, we might testify about it in court?"

"It wasn't something I was thinkin' about," Dingo answered.

"Why not?"

"I don't know. It just never crossed my mind, I guess."

"O'Riley? What were you thinkin' about? Why did you do it when you knew we were right there, watching you?"

"I don't know," O'Riley said. "It didn't mean anything. I mean, hell, like Dingo said, we done kilt so many now, what's another one, more or less?"

"Goxando? What do you say about it?"

"Kill girl is easy," the breed said. "Like kill bug."

"I have no more questions," Delilah said.

"Are you ready for your . . ." Slocum looked over at Danielle. "What's it called when they sort of sum everything up?"

Danielle smiled. "Summation," she answered.

"Yeah, summation. Are you ready for your summation?"

"Yes," Delilah said. "Your Honor, you heard me ask every witness if he was looking right at the prisoners when the girl was killed, and every witness said that he was. Then you heard me ask the prisoners why they killed the girl when we were looking right at them, and they all said it didn't matter to them that we were watching. Dingo said he couldn't count the number of people he had killed, because it was no different from relieving himself. O'Riley said killing didn't mean anything, and Goxando said he could kill a human being as easily as he could kill a bug.

"When I asked Danielle what it took to be not guilty by reason of insanity, she said that a person had to be incapable of telling right from wrong. I took that as meaning that at the time of committing the act, the person doing it must be suffering from such a lack of reason, and have such a diseased mind, that he doesn't realize what he is doing is wrong.

"Clearly, if Dingo cannot count the number of people he has killed, if O'Riley says killing means nothing to him, if Goxando says killing a human is as easy as stepping on a bug, those three men are suffering from that defect of reason. They didn't know that what they were doing was wrong, and if they didn't know it was wrong, then they must be insane. If they are insane, Your Honor, they cannot be guilty. And, as to Dingo's admitting that he killed Kathy, I would suggest that what he said in the wagon, while clearly trying to agitate us, is not the same thing as making a confession from the witness stand. And I would remind you, Your Honor, that when Danielle asked if he really did kill Kathy, he refused to answer.

"Defense rests."

Delilah sat down and, for a long moment, everyone was quiet. Finally, Slocum stroked his cheek, then looked over at Danielle.

"Prosecutor," he said. "I'm going to give you five minutes to prepare your summation. And I warn you, the defense has made a powerful case for these men. You had better be good. You had better be damned good."

19

During the five-minute recess, Danielle walked down to the river to dip her cup into the water. As she drank the water, she looked back up the slope at the "court" that was assembled there. She looked at Percy Keith, a bullet-scarred, bandy-legged man who, but a week ago, was lying behind the stable, passed out in a pile of manure. He was still suffering some from his long bout with the bottle, but she could sense about him a new determination, brought about by the self-respect Slocum had given him.

She looked at Slocum, who was surely one of the most fascinating men she had ever known. He had constructed a town and a court from whole cloth, and despite its rather unorthodox makeup, she believed that in many ways, this court was as impressive as any court in which her husband had ever pleaded a case.

Delilah and Marie were whores, but on this occasion they had both risen to meet the demands made of them. Delilah was arguing her case as effectively as any lawyer could, and Marie's meticulous minutes of the proceedings was the one thing that kept what they were doing from becoming a common lynching.

And finally, there were the three defendants. Surely God had never allowed more despicable creatures to walk the face of the earth. And it was now her responsibility to see to it that they never killed another innocent person. She knew that they wouldn't, Slocum had made it clear that they were going to die, but, in order to allow everyone to leave this place with a clear conscience, she was going to have to refute Delilah's summation. And, as Slocum said, Delilah's summation had been unexpectedly strong.

"Is the prosecution ready for summation?" Slocum called.

"I'm ready, Your Honor," Danielle replied. She slipped her cup back into her saddlebag, then walked back up the sandy slope to address the court.

"Your Honor, members of this court, that these three men are guilty, there can be no doubt. We are in a unique position, perhaps never before enjoyed by any court, of having been eyewitnesses to the very crime for which we are charged to try these men.

"Each of us, with our own eyes, watched the horrible murder of poor little Verity Dixon. We have our own knowledge of this act forever burned into our minds by sight . . . and, through our testimony, we have shared these visions with each other. This sharing was important, because now we are all certain that we saw what we saw.

"And, if our own eyewitness accounts weren't enough, we have heard the prisoners condemned by their own words. They have admitted killing Verity Dixon. In addition, Dingo has admitted, if not in a formal confession, then certainly in a believable dialogue, to the murder of Kathy Caulder.

"Also, though they do not stand accused in this court of other criminal acts, we have heard from their own mouths the most outlandish tales of evil and perfidy one can possibly imagine. They have boasted of murders and rapes and obscenities that boggle the senses.

"In their defense, counsel has suggested that these men might be not guilty by reason of insanity. I think it is important to point out here, that, even in defense, no attempt has been made to deny the commission of this crime. They are guilty of all that we have seen and not seen, heard and not heard, and as such, are an abomination to the laws of nature and man.

"So, with that it mind, it now seems proper and fitting to disallow the plea of insanity in order to find these men guilty as charged. But how can we find them sane? For what sane man could commit such horrendous crimes with such lack of passion?

"The answer is . . . no man could, if we gauge sanity by the standards of moral men. But these men aren't moral, and the only test of sanity we must hold up to the light is whether they were men of reason when they committed the crimes. Reason . . . for that is the important thing to consider when deciding whether a defendant is legally insane. Were these men of reason? Or were they totally irrational?

"I call your attention to a remark made by Angus Dingo when we first located them at their cabin.

" 'If you do not leave,' he said, 'I will kill the girl.' Your Honor, I want you to gauge the full impact of that statement. Dingo threatened to kill the girl if we didn't leave. His reason for that threat, and I repeat the word, *reason*, was to force us to leave. He was aware that the threat to kill the girl was one that would disturb us. He could not reason such a thing unless he had the *tool of reason* in the grasp of his mind. He could not threaten, if he was not aware that killing was wrong.

"Therefore, Your Honor, I submit that Angus Dingo, Kelly O'Riley, and Pablo Goxando were fully in possession of reason at the time we surprised them in their cabin. I furthermore submit that they were completely aware of right from wrong, and knew that killing the girl was a heinous act that we would deplore.

"If you accept this logic, then you must declare the defendants sane at the time of the killing. And, Your Honor, if they were sane at the time of the killing, they stand condemned by the collective accounts of the eye-witnesses, and by the words issued from their own mouths.

"If justice is truly to be served in this court of ours, if truth will prevail out here on this lonely sandbank, there can be only one verdict rendered toward each defendant. That verdict, Your Honor, is guilty, guilty, and guilty. And the sentence, should they be found guilty, can only be death, and death by hanging.

"The prosecution rests."

"There will be a brief recess while I deliberate," Slocum said.

Percy, Marie, and Delilah walked over to Danielle. All were smiling at her.

"Oh, my," Delilah said. "Your husband was right. You would have made one fine lawyer."

"Listen to who is talking," Danielle said. "Your argument was brilliant. Especially given what you had to work with. I have to confess, you caught me way off-guard. I had no idea you would be able to mount any kind of defense for these men."

"Yes, well, I'm glad you were able to knock it down."

"I don't know that I did knock it down," Danielle said. "The judge hasn't given his verdict."

"If he doesn't find them guilty, I'll personally knock him in the head," Marie said. The others laughed, and were still laughing when Slocum came back to join them.

"The court will come to order," he said.

All eyes turned toward him.

"Angus Dingo, Kelly O'Riley, and Pablo Goxando, stand before the bench."

Percy stood the three men up, then positioned them before Slocum.

"I find all three of you men guilty as charged, and I sentence you to be hanged by the neck until dead. Sentence is to be carried out immediately. Percy, help me get their sorry carcasses onto the back of the wagon."

"No!" Dingo shouted. "You can't do this!"

"The issue has been settled," Slocum said.

Protesting every inch of the way, the three outlaws were put on the back of the wagon, then the wagon was moved into position under the tree. Slocum and Percy threw ropes over the limb, then tied and looped nooses around the necks of the condemned trio. All was in readiness.

"Have you men any last words?" Slocum asked, looking up at them. He stood on the ground with his feet set wide apart.

"Please, no!" Dingo shouted. "Don't do this! I don't want to die! I don't want to die!"

"Dingo, you cowardly son of a bitch!" O'Riley said. "I can't believe I've wasted all this time with a pissant like you. Lash them horses, Slocum. I want to get down to hell in time for supper." O'Riley began laughing, a wild, hideous laugh.

"No! No!" Dingo yelled.

Pablo Goxando gritted his teeth and said nothing.

Slocum slapped a rope's end against the team, and the horses jerked forward. The ropes pulled the three men off the back of the wagon, choking Dingo's shrieks off into a death rattle. The last few barks of O'Riley's laughter echoed back from the hills, as if coming from hell itself.

It was deathly quiet, save for a creaking sound as the men turned slowly at the end of the ropes. It had been nearly five minutes since the horses bolted, almost four minutes since the last twitch from any of the bodies.

"Back the wagon up here," Slocum said. "I'm going to cut them down."

"We going to bury them?" Percy asked, as he climbed up onto the wagon seat.

"No. We're taking them to Pinedale. Marie, I hope you kept good minutes. That's about the only thing that will keep us out of jail."

"I wrote down everything," Marie said.

Judge Daniel Heckemeyer sat in his chair, reading the ledger book Slocum had given him. Slocum was standing at the window of the judge's office, looking down toward the center of town. Several of the town's citizens were gathered in the middle of town, watching a horseshoe-pitching contest between Andrew Dobbs, the champion of Boulder, and Jimmy Wyatt, the champion of Pinedale. The winner of this contest would go on to Cheyenne for the state championship, and, even though this contest was taking part in Pinedale, both men had their supporters on hand, as evidenced by the loud cheers that followed each clang of the horseshoe against the post.

Slocum left the window and sat down to watch Judge Heckemeyer. The judge had been reading in silence for several minutes now.

Another clang and cheer floated in through the open window, though Slocum had no idea who it was for.

Finally, with a sigh, the judge closed the book and set it down.

"What in the world made you think you could bring a town into existence, just by declaring it so?" the judge asked.

"Towns have to get started some way, Judge," Slocum replied. "How else are they started, if people don't start them?"

"An application must be filed in the county seat," the judge explained. "Then it has to be approved by the presiding judge."

"Who would that be?"

"Me."

"I see," Slocum said.

"You didn't do that."

"No."

"Therefore the town of Verity does not exist, and did not exist when you conducted this . . . trial and execution."

"I guess not," Slocum agreed.

"That means that you are all guilty of conducting a lynching," the judge said.

"No, not all of us," Slocum answered, holding up his hand. "I'm the one that pushed this through. If you are going to find someone guilty, find me guilty."

Judge Heckemeyer opened the middle drawer of his desk, then pulled out a form. "What was that name you chose? Verity?"

"Yes."

The judge filled in a few blanks. "Good name for a town," he said. "Sign here."

"What am I signing?" he asked, even as he signed where the judge indicated.

"You are signing a request for incorporation of the town of Verity, Wyoming. You might notice that this application is back-dated." Judge Heckemeyer signed his own name to the form. "The town of Verity now exists, and, by court order, has existed since the date of your voting it into being."

"That means it wasn't a lynching?"

"Barely so. The truth is, I don't think that, even with an approved incorporated town, that what you did was legal," Judge Heckemeyer said. "But it at least makes it murky enough that nobody is going to want to go into it. And speaking from my own point of view . . . if that was the only way we could rid society of those bastards, then I say good riddance."

"Thanks, Judge."

"Slocum?"

"Yes?"

"I wouldn't advise trying anything like this again."

That night, Slocum was lying in bed in the room he had taken in the hotel. Danielle was standing in the window of the room, looking down on the town. She was totally nude and her body shined silver in the splash of moonlight.

She chuckled softly, then looked back toward the mussed bed where Slocum lay, as nude as she.

"Now, why would I want to advertise when I've got all that I can handle, right here?" she asked. She walked back over to sit on the edge of the bed. "John, you think Marie and Percy were serious about making a real town out of Verity?"

"Could be," Slocum said. "Their share of the reward money is enough to give them a start."

"Marie and Percy getting married," Danielle said. "Who would've thought?"

"It happens," Slocum said.

"Do you think it will ever happen to you?" Danielle asked.

Slocum let out a long, slow breath. "Danielle, I'm not the kind of man who could ever let himself even think about such things."

"No, I suppose not. And I'm glad," Danielle said, brightly.

"Glad?"

"Well, just think, if you were married, you wouldn't be here right now, would you?"

"No."

"And if you weren't here . . . this wouldn't be here either." She wrapped her hand around Slocum's cock, which, though expended from earlier activity, was now showing signs of reawakening.

"No, that wouldn't be here either," he said.

"And I couldn't do this," Danielle concluded, bending over to take him into her soft, velvety mouth. She worked the crown over with her tongue until, once again, he was throbbing with need. Then she raised up to look at him. "Could I?" she asked.

Gently, Slocum put his hand on the back of her head and guided her down once more.

"Danielle," he said in a husky voice. "You talk too much."

Watch for

SLOCUM'S DISGUISE

285th novel in the exciting SLOCUM series
from Jove

Coming in November!